Under One Gosport Roof

Under One Gosport Roof

David Gary

CHAPLIN BOOKS

www.chaplinbooks.co.uk

This is a work of fiction. Although the novel uses real locations, its characters and events are solely the invention of the author and any resemblance to any person, living or dead, is purely coincidental.

Front cover illustration: Wendy Saunders

ISBN: 978-1-911105-61-9

Chaplin Books
75b West St
Titchfield PO14 4DG

I would like to thank Mabel Gary who provided me with the title of this novel, and Lesley Meenaghan who helped me with research into online dating. Thanks also to the cover artist Wendy Saunders.

CHAPTER ONE
Right Said Fred

Hardy was moving furniture again. Dragging it across the floor mainly, rather than doing a manly pick-up-and-place job. But why did he keep needing to do it, Joyce asked herself? Why couldn't he just settle? She thought of banging on the ceiling with a broom but decided against it: there had been enough bad feeling between the two of them without creating even more.

Joyce's husband of forty years was now occupying the upstairs part of their small house and she was occupying the downstairs. She had her own toilet downstairs but still needed to go upstairs into Hardy's territory to use the bath or shower. He agreed they should get builders to put in a proper shower-room downstairs; that way she would not have to make an 'appointment' with him every time. It was early days, however – their 'arrangement' of living separately but under the same Gosport roof was only a few days old, and there were still lots of things that needed sorting out.

This separation had not been as easy as Joyce originally thought it would be. She was unsure what Hardy thought of it: he had seemed just as unhappy with the state of their marriage as Joyce was, and even now constantly referred to her as the 'dragon'.

"We don't need a toaster in this house," he often said. "You can toast bread from ten yards with your breath." He clearly thought this was funny, but the joke had worn thin over the years.

She had felt unloved in her marriage from its early days. She had never got on with Hardy's father who had made unwelcome advances towards her. When she complained to Hardy about it, he had refused to intervene, saying his father was only messing about. It wasn't until the father's funeral that she felt able to mention it again .... and only Joyce would think that the funeral was the right time to have such a conversation. Thankfully, they were distracted by Hardy's frail aunt, who was standing so close to the freshly dug grave in order to launch her flowers onto the lid of the coffin as it was lowered that she nearly toppled in.

"Blimey!" exclaimed Joyce. "That would have brought a whole new meaning to BOGOF – '*bury* one, get one free'."

"Not quite the place is it?" Hardy had responded, acidly, though others around her were laughing.

Even just four years into their marriage, it was beginning to stale: Joyce was finding Hardy boring, so she had started flirting with other men. What really doomed their relationship was that Joyce had got off with a guy at a trade 'do', leaving Hardy to return to their hotel room alone. She had returned at four in the morning and although Hardy had quietly sobbed himself to sleep, he had pretended not to care and had turned away from her. The marriage was not the same after that.

After forty years, she had wanted a divorce, but the financial disruption of selling the house outweighed the misery of their relationship. At least she was no longer sleeping with him. They had moved a single bed downstairs from the spare room, thus giving Hardy a lounge upstairs. They were were not even eating together, or watching television together, or shopping together. But they still went to church together, and they were going to their friend Bert's funeral together tomorrow.

The doorbell rang. Hardy shouted down the stairs:

"It's for me, I think."

"What do you mean, you think it's for you? No one ever comes here for you."

"It's a delivery, it's a parcel, if you must know."

"What, for you?"

"Yes – just open the door, can't you?"

Sure enough, a man was standing at the door with a large parcel addressed to Hardy. It was on a sack truck, but the man just dumped it at the front door. It was heavy, so heavy Hardy had to drag it up the stairs one step at a time, there being no handles or anywhere to get a grip. At one time he could screw a nut onto a bolt nearly as tightly as using a spanner but over the years his hands had lost their vice-like grip.

Having witnessed the delivery, Joyce was now out of her mind with curiosity. Hardy suspected that she would be, which of course gave him great enjoyment. He knew her well enough to know that any event over which she had no control over would eat away at her. This was a situation he found rather satisfactory.

She wondered what could possibly be in a parcel of that size and weight. She thought back to just two days ago when she had wanted her large Victorian wardrobe brought downstairs into her new bedroom. Hardy had got it stuck between the stairs and the landing. At this point the wardrobe was resting on his leg, so he could neither go up nor down. Joyce ran round to Fred next door to see if he could help; he seemed somewhat bemused that it was coming downstairs for no apparent reason. Hardy and Fred thought for a while – clearly, Hardy needed freeing from his trapped position before they could do anything. Joyce was tempted to start singing 'Right Said Fred' but thought it wouldn't go down too well. In the end, Fred took the whole weight of the wardrobe for a couple of seconds, enough time for Hardy to get his leg out. That had the effect of the wardrobe sliding unguided down the stairs, with Hardy desperately trying to grab it before it ran Fred over completely. But Fred managed to hold onto the banister with one hand and arrest the progress of the enormous piece of furniture with his leg. This impressed Joyce, and spurred her into action, changing from a passive onlooker to a someone involved in the operation. It did need all three of them - it was very heavy, but because Hardy clearly didn't have the strength he used to have, the wretched thing had to be man-handled through the door of the lounge, at which point Fred noticed the bed. He must have put two and two together, and couldn't wait to get back next door and relate all this to his wife. Both Joyce and Hardy realised that one way or another, this 'secret' was going to be difficult to keep under wraps.

Joyce reasoned that Hardy never bought things online, so why would he start now? If he had bought this parcel online, this was one steep departure from his usual modus operandi. He had always displayed a distinct fear of anything relating to technology. The thought of buying something from what he called these 'shady online dealers' had been abhorrent to him. So either he had changed beyond recognition in this short time, or he had been out to a shop and arranged the delivery. Both options amazed Joyce.

She heard the rip of sticky tape being torn from the parcel, the sound of cardboard being removed, and she heard the odd 'bloody hell' as – true to form – Hardy encountered part of the package that seemed impossible to unpack. It was with great frustration that she wasn't able to hang around to find out more, but she needed to leave the house for an appointment at the opticians on Stoke Road. She tried to think of a reason for going upstairs, but could find no excuse, so reluctantly she left the house.

It was about two hours later when she inserted the key into the front door. The sounds that greeted her shocked her to her very core. Hardy was grunting rhythmically, and after each grunt there was a gentle sigh. She could even hear him breathing very heavily.

My God, she thought, he's wasted no time whatsoever – he's got a woman up there, I swear it! How dare he, how bloody dare he? They had only just separated their lives – he could have waited a decent time. The fact that he hadn't touched her in years shouldn't have anything to do with it, he wasn't that desperate, or at least he had never shown it.

"Hark at them!" she muttered to herself.

"Disgusting," she said, even louder, partly in the hope that the love-making couple would hear her. She assumed the least they could do, on hearing that she had returned home, was to stop the noise. Maybe they were so absorbed that they hadn't heard her?

It was five minutes before it stopped, which in itself marginally impressed Joyce. What should she do? Should she now shout up to him? How would that come over? If she did it properly, it could be construed as a caring thing to do, she thought.

"Are you alright, Hardy?" she enquired up the stairs.

There was a pause before Hardy replied.

"I'm fine, just a bit out of breath," he replied.

It was the breakthrough she needed. At the same time, she was taken aback at the audaciousness of his response.

"Why, what have you been doing?" she said, innocently.

Hardy was aware that Joyce was boiling over with curiosity. The conversation was difficult, shouting up and down the stairs, so Joyce moved a little way up, hoping she would catch a glimpse of a female leg, or even perhaps clothes lying on the floor. But no, she could see nothing like that; she needed to be further up than that.

"I need the loo," he replied. "Back in a minute."

Joyce knew he always needed the loo when he was cornered; when she had caught him out at something, the loo seemed to be his safe area. She caught a glimpse of him as he rushed along the landing. He had a greying white vest on, he was sweating, his hair was dishevelled, he was red, and he had on a pair of old blue shorts that had not seen an iron in years. My God, she thought, who could possibly fall for that?

The temptation was too much; she ventured up another five steps, enough to take a sneaky look through the open bedroom door, expecting to see some 'tart'. Instead, there it was: a brand new rowing machine. It suddenly all made sense: the grunts were when he was pulling, and the moaning sound was the whir of the resistance wheel.

Joyce almost laughed out loud, partly from relief. Of course he didn't have a woman – why would he? And if he did, he would probably have to pay for it, she thought rather nastily.

She retreated quietly back down the stairs, remaining undetected by Hardy. While it was comical to a degree, it did also worry her a bit. Why had she felt like that – disgusted but almost jealous? After all, she had effectively ended the relationship. She was confused. He was now his own man and his life was nothing to do with her any more, she told herself. Yet it seemed feelings for the damned man persisted.

On top of these questions, she also wondered what on earth had come over him. Why was he suddenly taking up exercise? He had never shown any inclination to 'body build'; this was quite out of character. But she supposed this might be a reaction to what was happening to him and his idea of getting on with his life.

It was at that moment that she realised that she too must make some decisions, that she should 'get out there' and take life by the horns. She still had chance to enjoy things without dull, dreary, moaning, old Hardy around her coattails. She should go out and meet people. What if she were to find herself a man? Meeting new people was tricky, because they had not yet gone public with their separation, but she could go online, she supposed. Joyce had heard of others doing that. At church she had been told that the lady who came from one of the 'extra care' places in Gosport had done just that and had met a 'nice' man.

"But you have to be very careful, you know," her informant confided, almost as if she knew Joyce might be considering the possibility. It was amusing at the time, but when it was pointed out that it wasn't about sex, it was actually money these guys were after, it became a bit more real. Joyce was convinced that she would never be 'conned' like that. For a start, she was not as desperate as some of the women that went on these sites, she told herself.

Joyce played with the idea. It had certain attractions: online, she could be who she wanted to be – it was an appealing fantasy. She thought of various false names and quickly decided on Felicity as a first name and Given as a surname. She noted them down on a piece of paper: they looked pleasing to the eye. Then it struck her that she might become known as 'Miss Given'. She crossed out the names and made up her mind to take no further action that day.

CHAPTER TWO
Goodbye Bert

The few people who were attending Bert's funeral milled around outside the church in the street until the last possible moment. Joyce and Hardy presented themselves as a couple to the assembled mourners, giving the others no suggestion that their domestic arrangements had changed so dramatically. Joyce was dressed entirely in black, complete with the hat that always had an outing at funerals. The hat always reminded Hardy of some large bird's feather, draping itself over her dyed blonde hair like a shroud. He had gazed at her as she'd waited for him at the foot of the stairs: she looked good all in black and his mind wandered as to whether, underneath it, she was wearing her red-and-black lingerie.

His own dress was standard bloke's funeral attire, white shirt and black tie with a dark suit. The suit smelt a little as he put it on – time for it to go to the cleaners, he thought. In the past, that had been Joyce's responsibility, but now, he realised, he'd have to do that sort of thing himself. Joyce also gazed at him and thought how much easier it was for men, seldom having to think how to dress.

The pair had walked to the church – no way was Hardy driving, just in case his idea of a drink afterwards was taken up by others.

"Look, don't show us up," said Joyce. "I know why we're walking. It's because you want to get into the pub over the road, don't you? Well, let someone else suggest it, and if you do go to the pub, I'm certainly not going with you." She thought she would lay down a few ground rules before they arrived. She had read his mind correctly yet again, Hardy thought.

Although Bert had been in his eighties, and could have been said to have had a 'good innings', the funeral was a sad event, mainly because of the circumstances of his death. He had died alone in his home, the home he had occupied pretty much all his life. He had not been found for days. Hardy felt particularly sad, and guilty, inasmuch as he felt partly responsible for Bert's suffering at the end.

After their protest on the Gosport Ferry – it was only two weeks ago but already Hardy couldn't recall exactly what they had been protesting about – he had gone to Bert's house to retrieve the protest banner. Both of them had hit the brandy bottle and became very much the worse for wear. Hardy had only left to go back to the protesters, because he'd had every intention to come back later with a new lightbulb for Bert's downstairs toilet … and also partly because the brandy bottle was nearly empty if he was honest … but Hardy never kept his promise. He never did buy a lightbulb, and he never went back. This was major source of shame for him. That he was also the last person to speak with and see Bert alive was also a major trauma.

Bert had been found at the table four days later by his neighbour, Mrs Burgess. The first impression was that he'd simply overdosed on alcohol. The man was, after all, in pain from his cancer and had little to live for. The one saving grace was that Hardy could confirm to the 'authorities' that he had assisted in the draining of the bottle, and in fact had probably drunk most of it. In the end, it turned out that it was Bert's cancer that had killed him: the brandy was just the finishing touch.

Hardy's feelings were not helped by the vicar, who was to give the eulogy. No one else had volunteered, although Hardy had given the vicar some anecdotes about Bert. In fact, Hardy had found out more about Bert on the afternoon of his death than in the whole time he'd known him. The vicar, however, had decided not to use many of the anecdotes, sticking to safe platitudes and a thinly disguised admonishment to the others concerning the events of that protest afternoon.

The organ started, brought to life by the regular young organist who provided accompaniment every Sunday. This time it was some piece of mournful material, heavily reliant on the bass clef. Joyce looked around, doing a quick head count: including her and Hardy, there were only ten people in attendance, most of those being members of their 'protest group'.

There was Olly, demonstrative, tall, his head always above others. His hair, once black, was now thin and mainly grey. He was a difficult man to converse with, he being totally logical, which could in Hardy's opinion be as annoying as dealing with an idiot. This time he had brought his wife, who was smartly turned out in a black dress and coat. She had taken no part in the 'protest', and while she appeared diminutive, she held considerable control over her husband. Ken, Sarah and Kenneth were also there - as they should be, thought Hardy. To their credit, on this occasion Sarah made it clear that she was actually with Ken by holding firmly onto his arm. Ken was still relatively fit compared to the rest of them, whereas Kenneth was overweight and found most tasks difficult. He was always busy looking after his wife, who had every symptom of every complaint the NHS had ever dealt with. Consequently, she was too ill to come today, pretty much as normal. Kenneth had attended alone today out of a sense of duty to the others. This little group had made it to the newspapers as a result of their 'protest', and when together felt almost like celebrities. That was a title the vicar was never going to ascribe to them.

"Oh, this is awful," Joyce whispered to Hardy. There was just no love there, she thought, and in this respect, Bert's funeral pretty much reflected his life. The starkness of the service was distressing: the man deserved better than that, and though the little group felt they should have elbowed the vicar aside and said some words of their own, it was hardly their place to do so; they weren't Bert's family.

Olly thought differently; he believed they were only there out of a sense of duty and of guilt, and he failed to see how they could do better than this somewhat reproaching vicar. Those feelings were being reinforced every time the vicar opened his mouth.

"Bert had been very stressed on the day of his death, and those of you here today will be familiar with what I am talking about," the vicar intoned. "Bert was a law-abiding citizen, that much we all know and we respected him for it. Yet, on that last day, the temptation to engage in revolutionary behaviour must have tortured him. This temptation came not from the devil, but from the very members of this congregation."

Joyce rolled her eyes at their mild little protest being described as 'revolutionary'. The vicar was beginning to sound like a Northern Irish Protestant fire-and-brimstone preacher, Hardy thought. The vicar had his black hair plastered down with some cream or other, in a very old-fashioned style. He was dreadfully overweight, which always made him slightly breathless climbing the few steps up into the pulpit. There was also something a little grubby about him, not dirty but not quite clean either, thought Joyce. The chastising was not yet finished.

"Bert was, in the end, relieved of committing a sin, purely because by his state of health. At least, you showed him that charity. At least the man died at home, in the home he loved. We may never know to what extent alcohol played a part, but the fact that the man was awash with it was not the Bert we all knew well. No, this temptation again came from a place least expected. The devil works in cunning ways and takes us when we are at our most vulnerable. Our strength to resist must always come from the Lord, and I do hope and pray that those seated here today can find again that strength through prayer and contemplation. I shall say no more, other than to pray for Bert's transition from this world to the next."

Hardy had thought that the funeral would give him – in what that phrase from the USA denoted – 'closure', and he could move on with his life. But it was far from that. He left the church feeling worse than when he had entered, and it showed in his face. He was also cross with the vicar. There was no need for further humiliation and especially in a holy place like that.

Olly had the same thoughts as Hardy. Never backward at expressing his feelings, he had made it clear to the vicar that Bert's funeral had not been the right occasion to trash a person who Bert obviously regarded as a friend, even if the vicar had not named him. Everyone knew who he meant. Bert, Olly argued, had had a choice: he did not have to participate in the protest on the Gosport Ferry, and he didn't have to drink all that brandy. Hardy did not force him.

Joyce had little idea that the events of that afternoon had caused Hardy to be feeling so cut up about it. She had been preoccupied, busying herself in separating Hardy from her. She had done pretty much everything, including dividing the knives and forks, giving him bedding and making a space in the freezer and fridge for his food, with a notice saying that he should get his own soon. New things she needed to do went through her mind pretty much every other minute, and it had happened during the funeral service. She would, she told herself, have to talk to Hardy about money, and that was not going to be easy.

No, Joyce was far too involved in her own machinations to notice anything Hardy said, but then perhaps that's what happens in separations - you're not meant to care about the other party. She had launched into the separation process the day after the fiasco of the 'protest'. She had made her mind up that this needed to happen after Hardy's disgusting drunken performance. Not only had his behaviour reinforced her feelings, she also felt it had given her the 'public sympathy vote', because the others had seen what he was like when he was drunk.

Now, she had just sat through a public humiliation of her husband. Her reaction, however, surprised her. She did not like it when Hardy was criticised by others - why? Because that was *her* domain.

"That was not necessary," she eventually said to Hardy.

"What wasn't?" he said, expecting to be criticised again.

"Him, going on like that at the funeral."

Was she really defending him? Hardy was lost for words.

One of the reasons that the funeral had been so basic was because there had been no way of finding any of Bert's relatives, if any existed; the responsibility for the arrangements had therefore been laid at the door of the local council. A Welsh solicitor employed by the local council was a man who, according to Bert's neighbour – a lady in her seventies – was far too hardened by the many cases he had dealt with.

"He was far too matter-of-fact," she had told Hardy when they emerged from the church.

They had now all reached the stage where nobody knew quite what to do. Did you just go home, or did you hang around making small talk? Bert was being taken to the crematorium by a hearse parked between two cars outside the church. The church was in a busy road in Gosport, with lots of small businesses operating in an area with little-to-no parking.

"Oh God, look at this lot." Olly gestured.

The narrow road was used by buses to get out of town, mostly heading for Fareham. Problems occurred when there was no room for one coming one way to pass another going the other way.

Olly was gesturing to the current gridlock, caused in part by the hearse. The hearse was pulling out into the road with a bus bearing down on it. The space vacated by the hearse was quickly taken by an older woman who was able to park her small Fiat with ease. The hearse was now trapped: it could not go backward or forwards, and to make matters worse, a bus was making hard work in the other direction.

Olly was the man to take charge here. His arms flailed about, calling the woman back to her Fiat.

"Oh, I think she's in trouble with Olly," Joyce observed.

"Bloody right too, stupid woman." Ken joined in. He still had Sarah attached to him, so was incapable of gestures.

Olly asked the woman politely to move her car so that the hearse could return, to allow the bus to pass. She eyed up the situation, which was getting worse by the minute: there were more and more cars, and in the distance, yet another bus. Olly was right, and the woman seemed to agree with him that she was the one who needed to sacrifice her parking spot to allow Gosport to move again. But poor Bert was still parked outside the church.

Olly took charge yet again.

"Oh my God, he's going out into the middle of the road," said Sarah. Olly's wife rolled her eyes in sympathy.

Olly raised his hand in an authoritative manner; he could easily have been mistaken for a policeman. The public are so weird, thought Hardy, when someone does something with authority: they just accept it, like they had in this situation. The traffic stopped in both directions and the hearse was able to pull out.

Hardy returned to the conversation about the solicitor, which had been interrupted by the gridlock.

"Well, I suppose it's just another job for him, isn't it? I doubt whether he can afford to get emotionally involved with cases," he said to Bert's neighbour.

The woman turned out to be Mrs Burgess, the same woman who had first sent Bert to the doctor's where his diagnosis of cancer had been obtained. She had kept a watchful eye on him, but always felt there was a cautious line to walk between being neighbourly and being intrusive.

"I mean," Mrs Burgess was saying to Sarah, who had detached herself from Ken and joined the conversation, "just because I didn't see a light for two nights, should I have gone in earlier? I knew he had no light in that downstairs toilet, so I bought him a bulb, thinking it would give me a chance to check on him without looking nosy.

And there he was, at the table. I knew it you know, as soon as I entered the house – I could smell and feel it. Oh, I do feel so terrible about this, the poor man lying there for several days."

"You mustn't reproach yourself my dear," said Hardy, feeling that it was actually her reproaching him. "You did more than we did, and we're meant to be his friends. And I get your point about when caring about someone's welfare becomes intrusion into their lives … it's very difficult to find the right balance."

He took the implied criticism on the chin. If he had gone back with that electric bulb as he had said he would, Bert would have been found that same afternoon. He might even have been alive later in the day, and medical assistance could have been called. But of course, Hardy had not gone back; he had lapsed into an alcoholic stupor.

"No sign of Kenneth's wife then?" Hardy enquired of Sarah, hoping to move things on a little.

"No, she says she is too ill to attend, and in any case, she doesn't like funerals."

"Oh," replied Hardy, "I dare say there's no-one here who actually likes them."

Sarah left it. She did not want to go into the real reasons for the wife's absence, taking the view that talking about bowel movements at a funeral would be inappropriate.

"Well this is a motley turn out, isn't it" Joyce said to the little group that had now assembled outside the church.

Kenneth was eager to point out that it was no fault of his wife's that she was unable to attend. His statement had his desired effect when Olly asked how she was now.

"Not good," he responded, "but then she hasn't been 'good' for years, has she? She has been a saint in the way she has coped and suffered."

No one really wanted to hear more of the saintly wife's suffering. No doubt she had, but it had been like a soap opera that never ends. Olly broke the awkward silence.

"So, what happens now?" he asked.

His question was answered by the appearance of a thin man with greying hair and thick spectacles who looked round at the group and asked that if they had been to Albert Blunden's funeral and had known the man well enough to help with finding relatives, would they please have a word with him. The man had a Welsh accent.

"Sorry, Albert who?" asked Hardy.

"Albert Blunden."

"Oh, you mean Bert! I've never heard him called Albert before and I didn't even know his surname was Blunden. So, are you a relative?"

"His name was on the bloody Order of Service for God's sake, Hardy." Joyce could not help herself, but her chiding did add to a sense of normality. Hardy ignored her – also as normal.

"No," said the man. "I'm from the Council – we had to organise the funeral and we are also dealing with the estate pending finding any relatives."

"I may be able to help you there," suggested Hardy.

"Thank you. Could you come and see me at the Town Hall? Here's my card."

The young man who had played the organ politely said 'hello' to the little group that had formed. Joyce recognised his wife as a regular member of the congregation. She was impressed that the wife had come too, so the couple earned a smile from her. That in itself was unusual.

Hardy was getting agitated. On the one hand, Joyce had warned him about going over the road to the pub. On the other hand, nobody was even suggesting it. He had hoped that at least one would have suggested it, so he could say it would have looked rude to reject the invitation, but no one did. Instead they had the usual from Olly and his wife:

"Well that's that then. We better be going."

That gave the others the idea as well; they all had to be going for some reason – there was to be no wake.

It had been a sort of reunion, but now it was over. Hardy and Joyce stood at the bottom of their stairs, both feeling awkward at what was going to be the end of their performance. They had performed well. Indeed, they may even have performed too well, because the other people in the small group were well aware of their inability to remain civil to each other for more than six minutes at a time. There had been hardly any bickering at all, to the extent that Olly had wondered whether one of them might be ill.

Joyce had decided that the separation be kept under wraps for the time being. She did not want to be questioned about it, and Hardy was happy with that; he too would find it difficult to tell people. At least they had no family to contend with. Hardy saw this whole situation as a failure on his part. However, he kept telling himself, it was not over: she had not moved out and the arrangement might turn out well. Perhaps they might even become friends again?

"I'll see you later then," he said to Joyce as he started up the stairs.

Her mood had changed again from the public display that she had kept going for the last couple of hours.

"Not if I see you first," she countered. An age-old response, but still one that hurt a little.

And so they parted, for another crazy day of deception and of staggering through with this new protocol. Joyce found it wearing; it was easier just to be her normal self and give Hardy verbal grief. She actually missed it.

CHAPTER THREE
A Chocolate-Box of Temptations

Joyce was determined to move on. She needed to make this arrangement work, but at the same time she saw this 'in-house' separation as a temporary measure before she could get her life fixed up.

Her mind was working overtime, and she was becoming aware that she had few friends to share her thoughts with. In fact, she had none. There was no family, which was both a blessing and a curse. A daughter, Joyce felt, would be an ideal confidante. She envied those women who were close to their daughters, and could discuss matters. But alas, that was not the case.

"I have to find a way where I can get out of the house more often," she said out loud, talking to herself because there was no one else. She found herself almost missing the arguments with Hardy, even though that was the very thing she was trying to rid her life of. There was no one to even ask if they wanted a cup of tea.

She needed to do something exciting, something that she had never done before to get over this malaise that she was slipping into. Joyce had a vision of her new life. The vision did not involve Hardy at all. She would live alone, and do what she liked when she liked. She had hated the routine they had got into. It was so boring. But her new life would be full of interest and full of men who she could converse with properly. Men who would be educated and sophisticated, who could discuss all manner of topics without flying off the handle like Hardy did. Joyce knew what she needed but was unsure of how she was going to get there. Even in this very moment, the only thing she could think of doing was putting the kettle on. She would change her clothes as well, to get out of the funeral attire. It was almost, she thought, as if the funeral was the line, the line that she could draw over her past life with Hardy.

The kettle rumbled in the background as she pulled her dress forward off one arm and then the other, and then removed the black petticoat underneath. She saw herself in the mirror, now dressed in only the black-and-red bra and matching pants. She thought she still looked OK, and it crossed her mind that she was wasting this body, that it should be caressed and be exciting for her and for someone else. She could not remember the last time that she had felt like this, and while temporarily pleasant, her brain told her it could also be dangerous. Again, she told herself of the perceived perils of a woman on her own.

"What's actually stopping me going out tonight?" she said out loud to herself again. The first issue was, where would she go? Could she go and sit in a bar, by herself? No way, she thought, here in Gosport it would be all round the town within minutes. Longer term, she could join something. What? A choir – yes, she could do that. A club, or an organisation that helped people – yes, but these things were longer term and how much effort would they take?

As she sat on the side of the empty bed, suddenly a sadness, almost a panic, spread over her. It came from nowhere. Suddenly she wanted company, intimate company. Not just the people she had just left at the funeral. She was very close to shouting up the stairs to see if Hardy wanted a cup of tea, but she told herself that she must not do that, not yet at least. He needed to understand that their relationship was over, and even inviting him for tea would give out the wrong signals.

She pulled on some jeans and a top, and made her tea. She would check her emails. There they were, eight of them since this morning: two from travel companies, one from some berk claiming to be HMRC. When did HMRC ever start a communication with 'Hi Joyce, Great news'? There was only one that she would open, and that was from their electricity provider – it was assuring her that because of her age, she was now classed as vulnerable.

"Huh, what a cheek!" she said. "But I must talk to Hardy about splitting the bills, or getting another meter put in." There she was again, speaking out loud to herself.

She brought up the internet, and pondered whether to look at the rubbish on Facebook, to read how somebody really enjoyed their breakfast, or someone who wanted yet another new petition signed. Occasionally there was a good joke on there, but that was rare.

She scrolled through, listlessly. Suddenly she paused: how on earth did that get there? There in front of her eyes was an advertisement for a dating site. She hovered the cursor over it, curious as to what adventures such a site might lead to. She drank her tea, then listened to what might or might not be happening upstairs. She could hear his footsteps plodding around. She wished he would put his bloody slippers on.

"He's doing it to annoy me, isn't he? Doing it deliberately," she said. She felt herself getting indignant and cross – even though the man was not in the room, his presence was there all the time. "This is intolerable," she said. "It's never going to work."

Then the footsteps stopped and she could hear the muffled sound of what she thought was his television. She went back to her tablet, and the advertisement kept calling her.

"Let's just see what happens," she said to herself. "After all, I'd been thinking about trying internet dating – seeing the ad feels like I'm being sent a sign." The site was free to join but required her to create a profile and provide an email address. She gave it some thought, and decided that it was too soon: she was not ready for stuff like that. What was she ready for, she wondered?

As Hardy changed from his 'funeral' suit into his day clothes, he became aware of a whiff from his old trousers - perhaps he needed to wash them? But not today – he could not be bothered to 'book' the washing machine downstairs and he certainly was not going to ask Joyce to do them, fearing they might end up round his neck. The smell always disappeared once they got warm anyway. Either that, or he became blind to the aroma. His suit was only brought out now for funerals; Joyce and he had not been invited to weddings for years. He took off his shirt, which was becoming grubby around the collar - it would have to go in the wash. His string vest hung on him; it appeared too big now, and was not as white as it had once been. Hardy's appearance had changed dramatically from the smart executive-looking man who had attended the funeral just an hour or so ago. He would have another go on his rowing machine; perhaps that would make him look more athletic and not so fat – he was determined to get himself into shape. He started grunting again. He heard her bang on the ceiling after about two minutes and shout to him that it was annoying her. That actually rather pleased him.

He was conscious that the machine took up most of his living room and, although he'd used it three times in the last few days, would he keep up the regime? Then it also occurred to him how stupid this all was, that he was getting himself up together for other women now, rather than keeping himself looking OK for his wife over the years.

Now he was putting on those old brown cord trousers that had once been fashionable, and a 'thousand miler' – an ancient polo shirt, whose collar allowed so much expansion of the neck that it might just as well have not been there. He was still panting and red from the exercise, and to top that was not bothering to shower either.

He needed to get himself something for the evening, so decided to go to the supermarket to get a bottle of Scotch. It was then that a huge sense of freedom came over him. He did a quick analysis of his situation: he still had a roof over his head, he still had the car, he still had – he believed – someone downstairs who would respond in a real emergency, but now he could watch what he wanted on telly, he could watch porn on his computer, and he could drink the bottle dry if he wanted. He could even pass wind without guilt, and she, who would otherwise cause a scene, would not be saying a thing. So it was with a light heart that he headed downstairs. He would rid himself of the guilt of Bert's death in time, and tomorrow he would start building his future.

Hardy's feet thundered down the stairs and the front door opened. Where was he going, thought Joyce, then reprimanded herself. It was no longer anything to do with her.

"Did you say something?" Hardy had heard her muttering to herself.

"No, no, just thinking out loud, that's all."

"Well, I'm just off down to Morrisons – do you want anything?"

"Oh …" She pulled up just in time. This was not how it should be. "No thanks." Although she actually did want some bananas.

"Suit yourself," he said – and with that the door shut.

Should she have said yes? Did she really have to break off everything? Her mind was still in overdrive, she thought about it morning, noon and night, and she had to face facts that she was really in a mess. Hardy seemed to be coping better than she was. This was surely the wrong way round, he was meant to be the one suffering. Perhaps this arrangement in the one house was too easy for him? Perhaps he was actually happy?

The idea of finding a new partner online was working on her. It had several pros … and few cons, the more she thought about it. One of the biggest issues, and she wasn't sure whether this was good or bad, was that Hardy would be aware of any guest she might choose to bring back home, and that would really get to him. On the plus side, it might actually get her out of the house and provide an interest other than this navel-gazing. Also, there was the remote possibility that she might fall for some dashing man who had enough money to allow her to move out of the marital home.

The problem was that she had no close confidante who she could ask for advice. She could not ask Sarah, otherwise the whole thing would be out in the open before either her or Hardy were ready for it.

All through the evening, she wrestled with the issues. She remembered what that woman had said to her about men being after money, not sex. She'd seen on TV programmes about women and men who had parted with money to fictitious people – fraudsters - and lost fortunes. She would not be as stupid as that, she told herself. Indeed, if she gave away only minimal information in her profile, she would be able to control the situation at her pace, and on the right site she would be untraceable. In any case, any unwelcome visitor would soon be sorted out by Hardy, who she would only have to summon from upstairs.

It was with some trepidation that she wrote her first 'profile', her sales pitch:

'Whilst just into my seventieth year, I am still very active and fit. I have just come out of a long relationship and am seeking to meet gentlemen of any age for outings, company and maybe more. I am interested in history and living on the coast as I do, I enjoy naval history. Photograph will be provided upon request.'

She read it out to herself and was not convinced. What was she actually saying about herself? What sort of man was going to be attracted to that 'advertisement', because after all that's what it was: the word 'profile' just dressed it up to make one feel slightly less pleading. She thought about the phrase 'and maybe more' – other women used it, but presumably it was just an invitation to sex. She was not sure she was ready for that at the moment. She tried another draft:

'Fit seventy-year-old woman, single and looking for excitement and affection. Interested in history and sport.'

She pored over both profiles and decided the first one was probably more fitting; the 'excitement' bit in the second profile might be interpreted wrongly. On the other hand, she thought, it might not!

She browsed through the site and decided to join the 'over fifty' section. There was no point in putting herself out there for nippers, she thought. She pressed the 'send' button. She had decided, in the end, to use a site that you paid to join, thinking that there would not be as many time-wasters on a paid-for site. Now all she had to do was to wait for the deluge of desperate men.

She also realised that Hardy might query a payment to an online dating site when their bank statement arrived. What was she going to say? Nothing she thought; he had no right to ask questions about her spending, which was another thing she had to sort out. They had always had a joint account: now they should have separate accounts. Hardy would have to give her some sort of allowance, because she could not possibly survive on just her state pension. Of course, this was where it all came back to roost - years of Hardy running the car repair business on the cheap, never paying into any private pension scheme because the business could not stand it, he had said. It was probably going to be hard work to get him to agree to any sort of fair financial arrangement.

For years when she had been doing some of the paperwork for the business, she had been suspicious about the cash side of it. Little things never made sense, the way Hardy always had cash on him yet had not visited the bank. The accounts did show them making the business marginally profitable, but they were never going to get rich on it.

She remembered him buying her a present, with cash from somewhere. She had not been pleased with either his explanation or the 'present'.

"I mean what husband with any thought regards a new hoover as a present?" she had said to the woman at one of their parts suppliers, who she often spoke to about invoices.

"He's a real romantic, isn't he?"

"He reckoned one of his customers had rewarded the extra work he'd put in on his car but –the cheek of it! – he had even wrapped it in gift paper for me. Talk about a let-down!" Joyce continued to complain to her.

The incident provoked her suspicion that Hardy had a secret fund somewhere. If there was one, she never found it.

"Why is he never short of cash?" she asked herself after looking at a bank statement. There had been no withdrawals in several weeks, yet he seemed to be able to spend at leisure.

She made a mental note to tackle him on this at some point.

She became alarmed when looking at her internet history to see she had visited seven dating sites. God, she thought, how easily one gets carried away. She reckoned it would be a good idea to delete that browsing history, on the off-chance that anyone else might see it – she was not particularly proud of such activity.

In a very short time, it had become an addiction: she kept returning to the site every couple of hours, in between viewing the ever-present rogue email advertisements arriving in her in-box. Like a chocolate box, there were temptations, chat rooms, more dating sites. They were all free, the ads said, but she wondered what traces they left on her computer. Could you pick up a Trojan Virus from these sites?

"I mean, what other way can these sites make money?" she wondered out loud. Her habit now seemed akin to smoking – you know it's dangerous, but you still do it.

There was one chat room that was free and anonymous, so she thought she'd give it a try. What could possibly be wrong with that? She entered the site under the nickname of 'older smouldering fem', laughing at her own ingenuity. She nearly came out again after four minutes. The pictures were not what she had expected. She had had no idea at all that men and women were prepared to put themselves on the worldwide web in such a graphic manner. "I should have nothing to do with this lot." she said to herself. "I'm getting off of here in a minute." But she continued to scroll down, looking at pictures she had not even imagined. She certainly was not going to put anything like that online. Then she saw it, a picture of a woman in her eighties, stark naked, and frankly not a body that should not be on public show. The nerve of it, Joyce thought – is there nothing taboo on here?

"I mean, compared to some of these women I have quite a good figure. Even some of these younger ones are not as good as me." She reassured herself, then laughed out loud when she saw a close-up pic that resembled Hardy. The face was not available, just a close-up of his belly, which was far from a six pack, and of course his genitals, which even Joyce recognised as being far from impressive. She thought what a laugh it would be if Hardy was doing the same and she recognised his genitals, which she was fairly confident she would be able to do. She chuckled to herself at the thought.

It was like a sledge hammer. Here she was having a laugh, but by herself and with not a soul to share it with. This sort of thing keeps happening: it was bound to, she told herself.

CHAPTER FOUR

An Act of Communion

Hardy ate in the cafeteria at Morrison's, a rather nice meal that cost him very little. Now he would get a bottle and perhaps some cheese to eat with it. He also bought a pie, an ordinary steak pie, which he had not had in years. This was going to be one hell of an evening. Probably he would need some Gaviscon, he thought.

"Oh gawd, the Gaviscon is downstairs. I don't want to do that, I'll get my own bottle – that's part of being independent."

"Pardon?" asked a bemused-looking older guy standing next to him in the booze aisle.

Hardy looked at the man before it dawned on him that he had been thinking out loud again.

"Oh sorry, mate, I was just thinking out loud."

"No problem," the man replied, looking a bit relieved that Hardy was not a total nutter.

Joyce was still mumbling to herself when he got back in, probably trying to sort something out on her tablet. She ignored him, but he suspected that would not go on for long. Her body language was all wrong. He couldn't put his finger on it, but there was something different about her.

He sat on his new armchair, and surveyed what had once been their bedroom. It all suddenly seemed bizarre: just a week ago the pair of them had lain in the same bed in this room, and now he was sitting there on his own in a chair staring at a blank television screen. He reflected on the situation: this might be just a sort of 'holiday' and in due course they would return to 'normal'.

Hardy had time to think and he had alcohol to help him think. Joyce totally dominated him and he felt that a period of separation like this might bring her to her senses, and that she would see just how badly she had treated him. He felt that she had no empathy for his situation whatsoever. She seemed not to understand the great disappointment that he had been unable to sell their business, or as she referred to it, 'his business'. When things succeeded, it was 'us' – when they failed it was 'his' fault. He had hoped to give the pair of them the retirement of their dreams, but while they were not poor, they were not rich either. Time had overtaken his business. Car maintenance, which had been his mainstay, had changed dramatically in the ten years before his retirement. Now, most cars were sold with the original dealership in mind, because expensive equipment was required to do services. His old-fashioned business was still servicing Mark II Cortinas, and the occasional VW camper van.

Hardy would tell people that he could remember the days when you could take a VW Beetle engine apart with just three tools – now it was done by computer. The Beetle engine was a work of art, in his view, under stressed, air-cooled horizontally opposed dual cylinder, no water to leak, no tendency for the engine to rip itself out of its housing. Then they brought out the Mini. That, to his mind, was the beginning of the end. He did well fitting sub-frames, but the engine was a pain to work on with little space for his sausage-like fingers. Things moved on again with the advent of the black boxes, the notorious electronic engine management system. These were the first of what he called the 'lock out' devices. Without a company's fault analysis computer, it became impossible to service the newer cars, and the business was no longer making the sort of money that would need to be shown in the accounts to sell it.

The other big running sore that had lasted most of their marriage was that they were childless, not out of choice, but because of a medical condition that affected Joyce. She had convinced herself that their childlessness was Hardy's fault and when she'd found out it was not, Hardy had gloated. That was nearly forty years ago, but Hardy still regretted how he had behaved, instead of putting his arm around her and telling her that he loved her no matter what.

Now it had come to this, and while he was currently OK with it, it had been Joyce who had called the shots. The only reason they were not fully separated was money. Joyce would never bring herself to move to anything more downmarket than where she lived at the moment, but if they split the money from selling the house, going downmarket was inevitable. She was never going to do that, he thought.

The bottle called to him. It was like a friend; it never let you down and had a funny familiar feeling of comfort. Even just getting the glass out was an act of communion with the liquid, and then the taste – bitter and violent on the tongue. It was quite illogical that it then became enjoyable. He could feel it go down, a warm comfortable feeling now, but the same burning sensation would be a disaster later on. He saw no point in buying expensive Scotch; this was the store's own brand, and it did the same job.

He knew his thoughts would become clearer with the help of the whisky. It was starting towards evening, and now – at the end of September – the nights were recognisably drawing in, and there was an autumnal nip in the air. This was going to be a long winter and a peculiar one, he thought.

The main desktop computer was upstairs. He was never sure that she didn't watch him in some way, being cunning enough to have some program that would track what he was looking at on her little tablet downstairs. But now, he thought, he could do what he liked on it, watch what he liked, because she couldn't say anything. He had set up a Facebook page about a year ago and had paid little attention to it, but today he decided to look at what people were saying. It was mainly advertisements, but then a post came up saying that local women were looking for men.

"Yeah, I bet they are," he said to himself. "There's got to be a catch, and probably a financial one."

Was he to spend the rest of his life like this? Was this a holiday from each other, and would Joyce eventually say "Let's not keep doing this, this is stupid," or would it go the other way? Now he didn't feel so free and easy. His mood swung again, and he thought about how surreal it was, pretending to their friends that they were still a married couple, but parting at the bottom of the stairs.

Hardy returned to his friend, the whisky bottle, surely it would all make more sense when his 'friend' swamped his brain. He put the telly on - he could hear that she had as well: they were obviously watching the same programme. Another Scotch, and then he'd heat his pie, and another evening would soon be over.

The TV was still murmuring at one o'clock in the morning.

"I bet he's gone to sleep in the chair again," Joyce announced to herself. She was in bed, but couldn't sleep because of the irritating, muffled sound coming from above her. She could do nothing but concentrate on the muffled sound coming from above her. Should she go up and check on him? After all, he could be ill or dead even.

"This is stupid, he is nothing to do with me now," she said, but still pulled the covers back in preparation for getting out of bed. Her big toe went into an immediate cramp. She had to bend down to grab it and stretch it. Her back made all sorts of noises as she did so, but eventually she got going.

She held the banister tightly, having put the light on at the bottom of the stairs. The TV got louder the closer she got to it, and some long-forgotten film was playing. She got to the position whereby she could see Hardy through the doorway, as the door was ajar. Sure enough there he was, slouched in the chair, mouth open and not a fly in sight. He was either dead or asleep. She debated whether to just turn the television off, or to wake him and tell him to turn it off, or just to go back downstairs.

She decided to just turn it off and of course, in doing so, he woke.

"Sorry," said Joyce, "it was disturbing me and I couldn't sleep."

"What?" said Hardy, bewildered and still half-asleep.

"So I just turned it off."

"Oh."

"I suggest you get to bed, it's gone one o'clock."

"Is it? Oh sorry, lost track of the time."

Joyce observed the whisky bottle, half drunk. It took her all of thirty seconds to revert to type.

"Oh that's it is it, pissed again and fell asleep in the chair?"

He didn't reply, he never did, and now he didn't have to. He knew of better ways to deal with her.

"Oh, you've got that see-through top on. Wow, still a bit pert then?" he drawled.

"For God's sake, get to bed." She turned from him, suddenly aware of her almost naked state, she scuttled off, back downstairs. She had provoked him again and not in a good way. And why oh why did she have to wear this gear tonight? It had lain unworn in a drawer for years, but tonight she had brought it out. She had given Hardy all the wrong signals. He might even charge downstairs rampant, unable to control himself with lust. But he didn't. She heard the toilet flush, and his bedroom door shut, and that ended the drama for the night.

The morning seemed like a new chapter; yesterday's funeral felt as if it was years ago and on a different planet.

"Hardy ... Hardy ... I need to use the shower this morning."

"So do I!" Hardy shouted back downstairs.

"Well you'll have to wait, I need it now."

"I was going to use the toilet!"

"Well, use the one down here while I have my shower."

"I suppose I could, if I can make it to the bottom of the stairs."

"And make sure you leave the pan clean, I'm not here to clean up after you now."

"For God's sake, woman ... well you make sure you leave the shower clean, then. Works both ways, you know."

Hardy started his way downstairs, while Joyce tutted at the bottom.

"Don't you come back up until I am coming down."

By now Hardy had had enough of being bossed about. However, his trip to the toilet was becoming ever more urgent, so he left matters at that.

"She really can't change, can she?" he asked himself, sitting on the loo. "It's in her DNA, I reckon."

Hardy needed to be fresh in particular today. He was going to the town hall to talk to the Council's solicitor about Bert, and Hardy's recollection that Bert did actually have a relative somewhere. The recollection came from his last conversation with Bert, on that fateful afternoon.

"The problem is," Hardy started to explain to the solicitor, "that I have to add a caveat to what I remember, in as much as we may have had a few drinks."

"What can you remember, then? I mean is the relative a female, for example?"

"That's right, yes, she is. She was, and maybe still is, a member of the Salvation Army."

"I have to say that is an extremely helpful lead."

"You said his surname was Blunden, which I never knew. Thinking about it, I knew a Blunden family years ago in the north of Hampshire." That was less helpful, thought the solicitor: he had found many Blundens, but none had led him to Bert.

"Bert was not clear as to her name – he thought it was Frieda, but he could be wrong."

"Well that is a chink of hope, I guess. I will get onto them and see if I can find anything more."

"Oh, I think she was more than just a member, I think she is one of their Officer people," Hardy added.

"Oh, that's even better – they are bound to be able to help with that because Officers are actually employed by them. The Salvation Army have quite an efficient missing persons section, so I think that may well be my first stop."

The solicitor thanked Hardy for the information and said he would let him know the outcome of any enquires. Hardy actually doubted that he would hear anything else from the man, and as he made his way home, he reflected again on the unfortunate nature of Bert's death. How could someone like that be so alone in the world – surrounded by people, yet with no attachments at all? Was it a decision that Bert had made for himself, or was it just circumstances? Hardy had once heard a person say on the television that 'loneliness' is a decision. He was not sure of that; he felt that a debate was to be had around that subject. Of course, he might well find out now, now he was on his own. It occurred to him that it felt strange not having Joyce walking with him now. They had seldom been parted, even though they apparently found each other's company so abominable.

Hardy understood very well that he was not really going back to an empty house. As he opened the front door, he got a whiff of her expensive Chanel perfume. This situation was a bit like leaving the European Union, while at the same time having some of the benefits.

"But hey!" he said to himself, "let's make hay whilst the sun shines."

So, to online dating he turned.

Hardy's biggest problem was the technology. In the past

few years he had relied heavily on Joyce to do things on any 'device' for him. He was even unsure as to whether his mobile phone was a smartphone or not. What did the term smartphone actually mean, he wondered? He certainly didn't want to ask Joyce, but in any case he didn't want to use a phone to do online datin'. He found using mobiles particularly difficult with his sausage-like fingers, even just dealing a number, and he had never found any sort of keypad on his handset. Joyce had bought it for him several years ago now, 'for emergencies' she had said. Well emergencies rarely happened, thank God, and so apart from learning to recharge it every so often, he was not a particularly effective operator.

Going to his computer, he punched in a search; he knew how to do that because he had done it many times before, looking for stuff he probably should not have been looking for. This search was simple, it was just 'online dating'.

There seemed to be plenty to choose from, some looking more dodgy than others. However, this was a world he was far from familiar with. Strange acronyms, strange language, indeed strange everything. Most had the same sort of format, but all wanted his email address. This would mean that if Joyce decided to check his emails, he would be exposed.

"But does that matter?" he said to himself. He was meant to be a free agent now.

The first site he went into was one that showed local women, allegedly. His desire was always subject to travel distance: he did not want to travel far.

He decided to tell the truth on his profile … well, not quite. He took five years off his age and described himself as 'active'. Another little lie was that he was single with his own house. He also declared that he had his own business, which he felt he could justify, but alas he had exaggerated the size of it and his role. Indeed, when he re-read the profile it looked like he was still working and in charge of his own string of garages. He chose a photo from about four years ago, taken on the beach in Southern Spain. Hardy was convinced that the picture showed him at his best. He looked somewhat tanned, and had been wearing a straw hat and an open shirt that showed the greying hairs on his chest. He was particularly taken with his smile in the photo, which he thought made him look cheeky and desirable.

He had chosen a site where you swiped 'left' if you didn't like what you saw and swiped 'right' if you did. If two people swiped right, the site put you in contact with each other. The relationship, if any, developed from there. It seemed that you could go through the menu and 'park' women you liked the look of, but if you wanted to contact any of them, then payment to join the site was required.

Hardy was reluctant to pay. He was always reluctant to pay for anything, but if he wanted to proceed then he had no choice. Of course, in order to get things going, the women who Hardy had 'swiped right' on needed to do the same for him. That was going to be the difficult bit. He worried that he had not sold himself well enough, though he saw no point in lying about himself, because if anything serious developed the truth would come out anyway.

The process was not as enjoyable as he thought it might have been. It raised questions in his own head. What sort of woman should he go for – mature, young, middle-aged? Should he read the profiles and go for ones with education, or business women, or professional women, or women who (in his terms? Seemed meek. That raised a further question: how Joyce would describe herself in her profile? Would she admit to being tyrannical, old, crotchety and rather friendless? Hardly! And that rather answered his question about the reliability of what anyone's 'profile' said.

After what seemed ages, he decided to try and contact three women, all from the same site, so there was only one fee to pay. He felt it was rather like choosing from a box of chocolates. He had opted for one from each age group, the youngest being in her thirties and the oldest being 'sixty plus'. The youngest, named Tittiana, had three children, which initally put him off, but on the other hand she had put up full-length photographs of herself, which he found to be rather a turn-on. Tittiana was keen to meet an older man, she said, so Hardy took the plunge and asked her. Her name must have been a wind-up, he reasoned – no one names their child Tittiana. He was tempted to ask her what she was called for short!

"Is sixty-three too old?" he asked Tittiana in a text.

"No, I like older men," she replied. "They are more cool and laid back."

"I am eager to meet younger women, there is still a lot of life in this old dog," he lied.

"I think u r sexy," she told him.

This was very encouraging, then reality dawned. How on earth could she think he was sexy on the basis of one photograph and a couple of texts?

"This is stupid," he said out loud. "She'll make me look an utter idiot. I'm old enough to be her grandfather. She's probably only after money." He decided not to pursue her.

The second one was in her late forties, still young compared to him. He had received a 'like' from her as well. This one was called Edna.

"Don't see that name very often these days," he said out loud to himself. However, the advantage with 'Edna' was that she was relatively close, living in Southampton. The other two were further away, and even though one of them seemed overly keen, Hardy put convenience above lust and plumped for local. That in itself, he thought, indicated that perhaps there were not as many hormones running around as there had been some years ago. It would also be cheaper on the fuel bill.

CHAPTER FIVE
Hardy Meets Edna

Hardy's mouth was dry, he had butterflies in his stomach, in fact he felt sick. Why on earth, he thought, was he doing this? Edna's main attraction had been that she lived not far away, but far enough not to be embarrassing if things went dreadfully wrong. He had arranged to meet her in a public place, halfway between Gosport and Alton at a pub called the 'West Meon'.

Hardy wondered about her name again. So old fashioned – as with Tittiana, he doubted it was her real name. He could not recall ever hearing a real woman named that, but there was something in the back of his mind, a TV programme from years ago called 'Edna the Inebriate Woman'.

The weather was not good, and he was early. In fact the weather was awful, but pretty typical for the last days of autumn. He sat in his car in the car park, rain lashing against the windows, which were slowly misting up. He wondered if she was here already, but thought he would wait at least another ten minutes before going over to the pub.

He looked at his clothes again. It had been something that he had not given much thought to until today. His wardrobe was not exactly trendy. He had decided on a suit that had not seen the light of day for several years. The suit was brownish, and he'd remembered that it went with a yellow shirt and green tie, if he could find them. The shirt had still been there, but not quite as easy to get on now, asking so much of the middle three buttons and not too good around the neck either. Perhaps he should give the tie a miss and look a bit more casual? He had wondered also whether he should shed his vest, his string vest that matched his string underpants, though Hardy had doubted very much that on a first meeting he would be declaring his underwear to her. Getting rid of the vest had given slightly more room for the flesh of his belly, but when he'd looked in the mirror, bits of flesh could still be seen between the puckered material and the buttons. No, he could not do this: even he was aware that was not a pretty sight. He'd decided to use the suit and shirt that he had worn to the funeral along with his black shoes. At least that suit and shirt fitted, and he could retain his underwear. He'd looked in the mirror and decided this was OK.

Last week, Hardy had found out that Joyce was seeing another man. She had not brought him back to the house but she had said to Hardy that she might do so at some point in the future.

"You be careful what you are getting into," had been his response.

"I know exactly what I am getting into, and in any case, it is not your place to give me any advice whatsoever."

"So who is it? What's his name?" Even on reflection that seemed a stupid thing to ask.

"I'm not saying anything more at this point."

Hardy had immediately realised he had made a tactical error.

"This is not a game," said Hardy. "We are now dealing with people's lives, including our own, and yet again you seem to just see it as a point-scoring exercise. This isn't just about you, Joyce, there are other people in this scene as well as you, like it or not." Hardy was annoyed by Joyce's attitude, the fact that she seemed to just dismiss other people's feelings so easily.

"Not at all. I need to see where it goes before I inform you of any future change in our arrangements."

"What you mean 'change in our arrangements'?" Hardy asked.

"Well, I don't know where I will be this time next year, do I? And neither do you, come to that."

Hardy's security blanket had been pulled off by those remarks. He had been provoked into thinking that maybe he had to do something about his own life, and it had been that little confrontation with Joyce that had provoked him into making this date.

He reflected, sitting there in the car, how that conversation had hurt him. He couldn't say that to Joyce, of course, because he did not want to appear weak, or as if he cared. But he did. It placed a whole new perspective on the issue. It made the separation appear more real.

By now, he wasn't quite sure that he even wanted to go ahead with this date.

He reasoned with himself: "Well, if I don't put some effort into life, what will become of me? And it could turn out OK. I may even get on with her. Come on, mate, let's do this."

There was no sign of any unaccompanied woman in the pub. He had booked a table and had told her that it was booked in the name of Hardy. He was still too cautious to give her his full name, but there was no one sitting at the allocated table. There must have been only ten other people in the whole place.

"There are never many in at lunchtimes, sir," said the barman. "Mainly older people like yourself."

Whilst it was true, Hardy thought it had been unnecessary to add the 'like yourself' comment. He took a half of lager over to the table and sat there, now not knowing quite what to do or where to look. He should have brought a newspaper, or be like the 'young' and bury his head in his mobile.

"Ah, perhaps I should check that - I might have a message from her."

Although he didn't quite know what he was looking at, it did give a good impression. His mobile phone in hand made it look like he was part of this crazy IT world we live in now. And of course, it gave him something to do, otherwise the half pint of lager would disappear too easily, and the last thing he needed was to pulled up for drink driving.

She was carrying more weight than she had appeared to in her profile, indeed much bigger than he had imagined. Her face, however, appeared younger than the fifty-nine years she had professed to be. Hardy could not help but notice that she was also very heavy-busted, beating Joyce in that department. He knew from years of experience that it was bad form to talk to breasts, so he made a conscious effort not to do so. He remembered a tip from other people on the site: 'put yourself in the other person's shoes'. Quite frankly, he didn't want to. She had obviously got out of her car straight into a muddy puddle, deep enough to flood her shoe, even with her high heels.

He stood to greet her. He was still a gentleman, after all.

"You must be Edna?" It was more of a question than a statement.

"And you must be Hardy." Her reply was more of a statement than a question.

She had draped a rather expensive-looking red coat over her shoulders to negotiate the journey from the car to the pub door. She now removed it, to reveal a tight-fitting black dress and white cardigan. Hardy fantasised instantly that she was probably wearing stockings. Sadly the mud on her red shoes rather destroyed the image. She saw him looking.

"Sorry," she said, "Got out of the car and into a puddle, but nothing I can do about it now, is there?"

"That's awful for you, your foot must be wet. Why don't you go to the ladies' and see if you can dry it?" Hardy was polite to the point of being sickening.

Edna agreed. Hardy thought if he wanted to run for it, this was the perfect opportunity to do so, and perhaps she thought the same. She could just leave by the other exit next to the ladies' toilets, and just never come back. There would be no harm done.

Edna did come back, and Hardy had stayed even though he was uncomfortable with the situation. After all, he was still married and if it was marriage she was looking for, he couldn't offer it straight away. Why has that even crossed my mind, he thought? We haven't exchanged more than ten words yet.

"Can I get you a drink from the bar, or shall we wait for the waitress?" he asked.

"I'm quite happy to wait for when we order the meal, and by the way, let's get this out of the way – I always insist on paying half. I never let a man pay for me on a first date."

Edna was clearly very confident and experienced.

"You will have to forgive me, but this is the first time I have ever done this, and the protocols are new to me." Hardy felt better somehow for telling her that.

"Oh right. Well I have to be honest, I've met six men on the same site where I met you."

"I take it they were not too successful, otherwise you wouldn't be here." Was that rude? Hardy suddenly wondered.

"They vary, but yeah, most of them have something that I find not particularly to my liking. You don't meet seventy-something-year-old men without baggage. And if you do, it rings alarm bells with me. But I am only looking for casual friendship really."

That came as a relief to Hardy, and also a bit of a reality check. She was obviously judgmental, and for God's sake, why should he replace one very judgmental woman with another? He realised he was looking for excuses to bail out.

"Yes, I understand that, you mentioned that in your profile."

She was gazing across the table at him before she suddenly said: "I am getting that you are not single – are you?"

"Why are you 'getting' that?" he asked, somewhat bemused.

"Well for a start, you have a wedding ring on, and secondly you are very nervous. I am guessing it's been a long time since you have done this. At the same time, I can tell you are used to female company because you are not staring straight at my breasts, which single men tend to do straight away."

The ring! How could I have been so stupid, he thought.

"Ah, the ring. Yes, I have been married, never really thought, though, of taking it off."

Edna was looking skeptical.

"I've dated two guys who both turned out to be married. They worked away from home, and I became suspicious when they were never available at weekends. 'Course, what had happened was that they wanted a bit of female company during the week, then at weekends they would return home to the wife and kids. You know, nice arrangement if you can get it."

"That's not me, though. I'm retired anyway."

"I thought you ran your own company – that's what you said on your profile. It's not quite adding up, is it?" she asked in a slightly aggressive tone.

This was turning more into an interview than a date. What was she getting so worked up about anyway if all she was looking for was casual friendship?

"Yes, I did own my own company, but I sold it recently in order to have more time to myself." Hardy knew that sounded lame, and he noticed that Edna's expression was turning more and more skeptical. This wasn't going well at all.

"So how long have you been divorced?" Edna continued the interrogation.

Hardy had not been ready for that question; in fact he had not been ready for anything much at all. He stared at her. She was not looking angry, more inquisitive. He had not answered her question before she quickly added,

"Look, I am trying to clear the decks here. I want to know what I'm getting into, and one of the red flags that wave to me is when I am with a liar. Now I don't know whether you are looking for a dingey relationship with benefits, or whether you're seeking a genuine relationship whereby we can comfort and support each other, and also spend nice times together." Her tone was earnest, not accusing. She hadn't finished. "At our ages, we all come with baggage, as I said just now. If you don't, then I don't want to know really, because you won't have any chance of dealing with me and my wants. Just be honest with me, because if you are not, today will be the last time we meet."

Hardy felt lectured and to a degree belittled. He was amazed at how hard she seemed, how matter-of-fact she was, almost like laying down the preconditions to a contract. Was she like this all the time? Was he even going to enjoy the next hour with her while they ate lunch? He hadn't come on a date to be cross-questioned about his life like this. That was swapping like-for-like with Joyce, even worse, because he thought he knew how to handle Joyce, but Edna was like a bull in a china shop.

There was a short silence before she said:

"Well then, do you have anything to add to what I already know?"

This was almost humiliating, but then he was used to that. He made a subconscious decision to plod on, even if he put the whole thing down to experience and called it a day later.

"I have been living apart from my wife for about two months now. She lives downstairs and I live upstairs - we still share the same house, you see."

Edna's eyebrows rose.

"That's a new one on me. How the hell does that work?"

"Well it's not easy, but it is practical, particularly as regards finance. But of course, it's tricky too, we have to set times when we use different facilities in the house, so she has a shower at ten past eight in the morning, while I use her downstairs toilet. Brings a whole new meaning to keeping regular."

Hardy had thought he cracked a joke, but she did not respond, not even with a smile.

"So, do you still mix socially?" she asked.

"Oh no. She hates me."

"Do you hate her?"

"Sometimes, but then at other times I wish we could just get on. I'll be honest with you, it wasn't my idea to live like this."

Was it a good idea to be so honest, he wondered?

"It seldom is - most men seem to do anything for a quiet life. So, if she suggested reverting back to the old arrangement, would you want to?"

"That's a good question. I haven't really thought about it - I am all over the place, to be truthful."

The interrogation continued.

"So, obviously this is your first foray into the dating scene. Do you think you are ready for it? I mean, what are you looking for from this date with me today, or dating with anyone come to that?"

Fortunately for Hardy, he was spared the need for an immediate answer when a waitress arrived to take their order. Of course, Edna was not ready to order: she had not even glanced at the menu, and one of Hardy's pet hates was when you had been given ample time to select something in a busy restaurant and the person you were with had not even bothered to look at the menu. She also irritated him by proceeding to ask lots of questions about just about every dish on the menu, taking several minutes to come up with a firm order. Hardy stuck to battered cod and chips and mushy peas. He had been told some time ago that the Queen never has peas because they have a tendency to roll around the plate, hence he felt safer with the mushy variety. He deemed it in order to comment about Edna's order.

"That was a marathon," he said. "You are obviously careful about what you eat."

"I'm careful about anything that goes into my body, and always ask questions."

The fact that she had said such a thing with what Hardy interpreted as a suggestive smile knocked him right off kilter.

"I am guessing," Hardy went on to say, "that you question all your dates like this."

"No, not necessarily, if they are just looking for a quick evening and sex with no ties then if I like them, I don't bother."

This was outside his comfort zone. He had no idea where this was going or whether indeed it was going anywhere. Yet in a rather sordid way he found the whole situation rather erotic. She was provocative, yet at the same time he felt she was playing with him.

"Do you and your wife still argue?"

"Just about every time I see her," Hardy replied with gusto.

"You see, that tells me a lot."

"Yeah, that we should have split up years ago."

"Naaah … I always reckon that a marriage can only be considered over when neither party no longer cares enough to fight."

Blimey, thought Hardy, this woman really has gone into things.

"See," she continued, "I am getting the impression that you don't know why you're here. You haven't worked out what you want from any relationship, and you are just going through the motions because that's what you think you ought to do. I don't even think you are looking for cheap thrills, either. In my experience, this is all too early for you – you need to sort your head out."

This whole experience was turning more like a visit to a psychiatrist. She seemed to be loving it, however.

"Look," she continued, "I am more than happy to eat with you and we can be pleasant to one another, but I think that's as far as I would want to go. You come over as a sweet lost soul, and before you reach out to other people, you need to find yourself first. Only then will you understand what is for you and what's not."

Hardy sat there listening. 'Find himself'? What on earth was she on about? But he did get it; this was going to go nowhere, she had made that clear. The odd thing was that it didn't seem to matter to either of them, and actually took away a load of tension. He had not been aware of it, but his whole body had been stressed, now he could let go because they were going to shake hands at the end of this meal and say their goodbyes.

Their meals were not long in coming, but her interrogation continued.

"Does your wife have lots of friends to turn to?"

"No, not really, in fact I can't think of one. Come to that, neither do I. I did have a friend, but he died about four months ago."

"There's something strange about a woman with no friends of her own sex. I always advise, beware of that woman." Hardy thought the warning was a bit late.

"When we had the business, we were with people all day – we had loads of social events to go to, and I suppose when we sold the business, it all just faded away. Thinking about it, we have probably kept people at arm's length. We see friends at church, but apart from Sundays and the odd social, we don't see much of anybody."

"I find it fascinating that you still refer to 'we'," Edna observed.

Hardy dropped a chip. He hoped she had not noticed, and certainly if she had she did not comment.

"Oh, don't read much into that, it's just habit," he responded. He thought at the same time that he would end this barrage of questions by asking some of his own.

"So you have never been married then?" he asked.

"No, never found the right man ... well, never found the right man at the right time. You know, as life goes on, more and more things need to come together for a meaningful relationship - firstly I need to fancy the guy, secondly he needs to fancy me, thirdly I need to be in a position to pursue the relationship and so does he. To put all those ducks in a row these days is quite a feat. I've only ever had one serious relationship, that lasted about a year. I never lived with him, even though I was round his place most of the time."

"So what stopped you marrying him?" Hardy asked, genuinely interested.

"Well, I was in my mid-thirties then, and I had just bought a flat of my own for the first time. I had worked bloody hard for it, and valued the place as my own. So I was reluctant to give that up but more than that, of course, he came with a complete suite of baggage, an ex who was giving him grief, and three kids. He just talked and talked about it. Not that I minded at the time, but I asked myself if I stayed with him, how long the angst would go on for."

"So you decided to end it?"

"Hell no. He did. He got to the point where he couldn't stand what he called my intensity. He understood that I actually enjoyed going over his problems, but I think in retrospect I may have actually stopped him burying stuff that he was not ready to examine. You can only do things when the time is right, you know."

Hardy was not surprised, and he felt that evidently she seemed to have not learnt her lesson.

"At the time, I had had little experience with men," she said. "I had looked after my mother since as long as I can remember. She had extreme joint pain with arthritis. As a consequence, I missed out on the normal teenage stuff. Much of what I knew about men had come from films. I didn't even have my father as a role model because he left when I was three."

Hardy's attitude softened a little. There were back-stories behind everyone, he thought.

"What happened with your mum?"

"She went prematurely into a care home, and died within six weeks. That left me with a huge sense of guilt. Was it me that killed her by putting her in that home, I constantly asked myself that?"

"I don't think you should reproach yourself – you'd done your bit for her over the years, hadn't you?"

"Of course I had. Everyone knew that, including me, but it still didn't stop me questioning myself. The thing was, I suddenly realised I was free, free as a bird. I had a good job and a few quid in savings. But I didn't have a clue what to do with that freedom. In a bizarre way that's a lot like you are going through at the moment, so I do have empathy with you, Hardy. I mean, you have now got freedom, yet cannot define it. Do you actually want to be free, or not? This is what I mean by having to sort yourself out."

Those remarks made an impact on him. It was clear she meant it. What she said seemed to come from the heart, and he had never had a chat like this in his life. He wanted to know more.

"So what did *you* do with the new freedom?" he asked. He half hoped she would have answers that he could model himself on.

"This is the daft thing. The moment I was free, I looked

to be tied up again. I went looking for men and to a degree, I still am. I had told myself that I had a lot of life to catch up on. Can you believe it, Hardy, I was still a bloody virgin at the age of thirty-two! I felt ashamed of it. But I kid you not, Hardy, it's not easy. Where do you find men, unless you have the guts to try and get picked up in a pub?"

"No, and you don't know what you are picking up either."

"Course you don't, and it's only slightly different with this online stuff. Most of the guys on there tell lies about themselves. But I did go to a DSS club with a girl from work and had my first affair."

"DSS?" Hardy queried, thinking it must be something to do with social security.

"Oh, sorry, it stands for Divorced, Single and Separated. It should have been called 'married guys on a night out, and married women looking for a way out'."

This was another new one on Hardy – he didn't even know these places existed.

"They were usually held in a hotel on a Thursday night, ideal for guys away from home, but for me at the time that didn't matter. In fact it was a plus, because if I had gone with a chap who had no experience, having had little experience myself, I think it would have been a right mess."

Hardy was again taken aback by the frankness of this woman – was there nothing she would not talk about?

"I understand that. It's weird, isn't it, that we get taught pretty much everything in life by those that know how until it comes to ... well, you know."

"Sex, you mean – why can't you just say it?"

Hardy ignored the question, like always when he felt threatened.

"Lots of the problems people have with sex, are a result

of poor communication," she said. "I was once told by a sex therapist that only about one in ten women ever tell their partners what is great for them in bed and what is not so good."

Hardy thought about Joyce, remembering back to when he was expected to understand everything about her body without so much as a route map. He was getting more and more uncomfortable with this line of conversation.

"I'm guessing you never met anyone suitable at these clubs you went to."

"Well, they were pretty much all one-night stands. I was stupid but, like I said I thought I needed to catch up on what I had missed, so I went feral."

"So where did you meet the guy you got serious with?"

"At work. He was my boss and he was getting divorced. I thought for a little while that he might be the one that I could settle down with, but now. I think I'm not sure I could ever settle down with anyone."

"Don't you miss not having had children?" Hardy asked.

"Oh God no, there's not a mothering bone in my body. But of course that's what you'll need to watch out for if you date too often."

Hardy was completely bewildered.

"I call them the bed and breakfast girls." Edna knew she could not leave it there. "They're women in their mid-thirties who want babies, but not a lifelong commitment to a guy. So they choose older guys like you - they get pregnant and marry you, maybe even not in that order. I mean, not wishing to be offensive, how long d'you reckon you got - ten years max?"

Hardy almost laughed at her 'not wishing to be offensive' when saying something completely offensive.

"Don't know, do I? No one does."

"Well anyway, the theory is that they get married, have a child or two, get all the financial security that marriage brings and then the bloke dies, leaving them in a great position."

"Bloody hell, how mercenary is that?"

"Is it really, if both parties are happy?" she queried.

"What about the child, not having a decent time with its father?"

"Never thought of that."

Bloody hell thought Hardy, there was actually something this woman had not thought about! Their meals were growing cold, and unsaid protocol dictated they should actually eat something. A period of relative silence followed. Hardy noticed that Edna picked at her meal, almost as if she did not want it. Little bits were pushed aside by her knife and only small selective portions actually entered her now silent gob.

He had been unaware of the fellow diners in the pub. He looked around him for the first time and wondered if they had all been listening to this rather frank discussion. She had totally drained him, to the point where he had lost track of time and place.

Neither wanted pudding, in fact neither wanted much more of anything. After just over an hour with her, Hardy felt worn out.

The rain had stopped as they stood together in the porch.

"Well I suppose this is goodbye." Hardy offered his hand to her.

She took it, and he felt a very feminine hand that obviously did little work. She had extremely long fingers, he thought.

"Yes," she said, withdrawing her hand. "I do genuinely wish you luck, you are a nice man, but I would slaughter you, I'm afraid."

Hardy laughed. "I will say this, for me anyway, today hasn't been a waste of time. I have learnt a lot about dating itself, and most of all I have learnt a lot about me."

"And Hardy, that's what's important. If I have helped in any way with your understanding of what is happening to you, then I can hold my head up and say that I have helped someone navigate this hostile planet."

He thought that was a bit condescending, but it didn't matter, she would be gone out of his life in a few minutes. With that, she was gone, and now he would have a good three quarters of an hour with himself in the car as he drove back to Gosport, to wrestle with what had just happened.

"Wow, what a woman!" he exclaimed. "I had no idea that women like that existed! I guess I should think myself lucky that she had such a handle on the situation. And that business with the babies – I'm going to have to keep my eye out for that." His conversation with himself paused while he thought. "But why not? I might enjoy having a younger wife, and it would really get to Joyce if I had a child!"

CHAPTER SIX

A Man of Class

Joyce was beginning to feel lonely, an emotion she had not programmed into her future life. Hardy was out again.

"He needn't think he's getting a life of his own, I'll kill him," she muttered. She scrolled discontentedly through the dating website; there had so far been no reaction to her profile, but then it had only been 24 hours.

She thought she'd have another try at a chat site, hopefully one a bit more respectable than the first one she had tried. This time she just scrolled quickly past the pictures that men had posted of their genitals to see if there was anyone who looked remotely worth chatting to.

'Older male looking for kinky UK woman' said one entry. Joyce stared at it. What actually qualified as kinky? Nothing ventured, nothing gained: she typed 'hi' and clicked the 'private conversation' box. After about three minutes a response arrived. It read 'asl'.

She typed 'I don't know what that means.'

'Age sex location.'

Every day is a school day, she thought. She lied and put '62 female England south coast.' Could she get away with claiming she was 62?

'I like older women.'

'How old r u and where r u?' She felt 'down on the streets' using the tech speak, as she thought it was called.

'so what u into babe'. She noted the lack of capitals and punctuation. This one was going to be difficult: she guessed he did not want an answer of 'sewing'. But what could she say? She had little idea regarding much of the stuff being discussed on this website, in fact she was beginning to think that the world had left her behind. "Enough of this thinking," she said to herself. "I have got to come up with something to keep him interested."

'I like to dominate men' she typed. God, she thought, where on earth did that come from? Hardy had often accused her of being naturally dominant. She had told him that she had not seen herself in that light, and that her behaviour was no different to any other married women that they knew.

'oh wow' came the response, then after a moment: 'ru strict'. Joyce was savvy enough to know that this guy was definitely kinky. She had no interest in that, even though she naturally preferred to be in control.

She was getting out of her comfort zone now, even though she had only been active for a few seconds. She was aware that she was feeling a bit panicky. She just turned the machine off, sat back and took a deep breath. That was quite enough for today, she thought. She would return to her television and the safety of watching 'Casualty'.

Several days later, she was getting applications from men on the dating site, and getting the hang of 'swiping right' and 'swiping left'. Several times she got it wrong and got messages from men she had meant to reject, but one of those messages caught her eye.

The guy had a profile on the site indicating that he was a musician who played classical Spanish guitar and was also an artist working in oils. At last, a bit of sophistication, she thought ... if it was all true. She had some doubts that it was, but thought it worth a go. His photo showed him with a huge smile, jet black hair swept back, and extraordinarily white teeth. He looked Mediterranean and was wearing a black shirt.

They started messaging. He said he lived in Teddington and that his name was Charles, (never Charlie).

'I live in Gosport,' she had responded.

'Where is that?' Charles asked. That annoyed her; she always got annoyed when she had to explain to people that it was opposite Portsmouth, at the entrance to the harbour.

'Gosport is a key defence area that supports the work of the Royal Navy in Portsmouth. Our claim to fame is that we are the largest town in Britain without a railway station, that dreadful man Beeching having denied us that privilege.' She looked at that before she posted it, thinking that it wasn't strictly true, but she always wanted to make a dig at transport links. Typing long messages was proving fiddly on the little keyboard of the tablet – she would have to learn 'text speak'.

'How do you get anywhere if you don't have a car?'

'We have to get a ferry across the harbour to a disgusting, ugly shed which Railtrack have the cheek to call a railway station. It takes 90 minutes from there to Waterloo.'

'Sounds fabulous, getting a ferry.'

'Yes, magnificent trip on the ferry.'

'Do you drive?'

'I don't have use of a car at the moment.'

'I don't drive either. Would need to use public transport if we meet up.'

She told herself that an alarm bell should ring then, that was too soon for her to think of meeting someone. She needed to speak to him on the phone first and she decided to tell him that. He agreed, in fact he seemed very reasonable and had so far not blotted his copybook.

She would rather ring him: it gave her control. She would ring him when it was convenient to her.

It actually did not take long. She rang him that evening when she could hear Hardy's television playing upstairs. In theory, Hardy would not be able to hear her conversation. She would use a landline and withhold the number – that was about the safest way of doing it, she thought.

"Hello?" It was almost a question from him, a gentle voice she thought.

"Hello, is that Charles?"

"Indeed it is, is this Newgirl?" Joyce needed to be careful – that was how she had presented herself on the site, and she also needed to remember the other 'porkies' she had told as well.

"My real name is Joyce."

"Oh, well hello Joyce. Thank you for ringing me. I didn't really expect it."

His voice was so soft she could hardly hear it.

"Oh, why was that?" she didn't mean to, but she sounded off-hand.

"Well, there are lots of jerks on these sites, just out for quick kicks, I thought you may be one of those. Lots of men pose as women."

"What on earth is the point of that? Well, I hope I have proved I'm not one of those. So, Charles, do you want to chat?"

"Oh yes, of course, we need to find out about each other."

"Right, so are you working still?" Joyce asked.

"Only when I have to - I sell my paintings otherwise."

"You sell them commercially?"

"Oh yes, I have sold two in the past two months - eight hundred pounds in one case and eight hundred euros for the other one," he told her.

She was impressed. A real artist: if this was all true, this man had class.

"What sort of paintings are they?"

"Mainly figure studies, although I have done some landscape. It is a painter's paradise here, because I live not far from Richmond Hill, which looks out for miles over Sussex. It gets crowded with artists up there on a nice day."

"Oh yes, I do know where you mean. I have only visited it once or twice, with Hardy."

"Hardy?"

"He was my husband at the time," she said, silently congratulating herself on negotiating the question without lying.

Joyce quickly put the focus back on Charles.

"So, are you single? Please be honest, because it all comes out in the end."

"Yes, I am single, I am divorced and I do have children, both of whom are grown up now. I have two sons, who both support themselves." He seemed to know that was important.

"I have no children." Every time Joyce told anyone that, it seemed to her more like an apology than a statement. She also noted that she was volunteering information, though Charles had actually asked for nothing. She put it down to her feeling nervous.

"You're not the maternal type, I'm guessing?" he asked.

Here was an enormous assumption. It was the usual programming, stereotyping, putting into a box - no children meant militant feminist. What did he want to hear, she wondered?

"We decided we did not want children," she said. "My husband now lives apart from me after a long marriage. Are you still in contact with your family and your ex-wife?"

"Yes, my ex is a classically trained singer, opera mainly, but she does other work whenever she can get it. Of course, that meant she was away a lot of the time, and I guess we just drifted apart. There was no real acrimony, and when she gets the odd solo part, I sometimes still go and listen to her."

To Joyce, this was all adding to the impression of 'class', something that she had been denied in her marriage to Hardy, or so she thought.

"In fact," he continued, "that's given me an idea that might be a bit of an ice-breaker. She is performing in Basingstoke's Anvil Theatre next Saturday - why don't you meet me there? I can get you a ticket and Basingstoke would not be too far for you to come on the train. It would be on neutral ground as well as in public."

This was another impressive offer as far as Joyce was concerned. He was being entirely open, and the fact that he was including his ex-wife in the scenario was also refreshing. There would be little threat in that.

"What time would that be?" Joyce found herself saying, quite eagerly.

"The performance is at seven, so why don't you get here for around five, and we could have a bite to eat in the cafe inside the theatre, and get to know each other a bit better. If you want to stay for the performance, that will be fine, if you don't that will be fine as well."

"OK then, I will see you at the theatre cafe at around five." Simple, she thought.

Pleasant farewells exchanged, Joyce put the phone down, shocked and bewildered at what she had just done. She sat back in her chair, staring at the ceiling, a mixture of emotions passing over her. She had just two days to think about this.

That is exactly what happened. She thought about it when going to bed - what's it going to be like? At breakfast; what's it going to be like? The whole day went on like that. She was screaming to tell someone, but the old problem raised its head – who? It even went through her head that she should tell Hardy, just for security reasons. "I mean if I get into trouble, he would still be the one the police would come to, and it could cause problems if he knew nothing about it," she reasoned with herself. Of course, it wasn't just about security: there was the pride element and the thought of 'getting one over' on Hardy.

She caught him going up the stairs with his bit of shopping on the Friday afternoon. He cut a weary sight; everything he did, he did with a weariness. He was stooped over, red in the face and looking troubled. But then he had always looked troubled.

"Ah there you are," she said in an almost aggressive way.

Hardy looked up, with 'what do you want?' look.

"I thought I ought to tell you, for security reasons, that I shall be out from midday on Saturday afternoon for quite some while. I am meeting a gentleman who is taking me to the theatre."

She waited a couple of seconds for the reaction. There wasn't one.

"I'm going up to Basingstoke."

"And what would these 'security' reasons be?" Hardy enquired, curious as to what game she was playing now.

"I just thought that as we still occupy the same property, you should know that I am going to be out for some time, and I thought you might show some concern, just as a fellow human being. Obviously I was wrong." It had not taken long for her defensive position to change to that of being passively aggressive.

"No, you're right I suppose, I would have been worried if I didn't know you were in when it was getting late. I mean you're not planning to stay overnight with someone, are you?"

God, it was so obvious he was fishing thought Joyce, and she wasn't going to give him the satisfaction of a definite answer.

"Well, we'll see, won't we?"

"Ring me if you do, then I'll know where you are."

"Well, I don't know about that. Why should I tell you what I am doing?"

"Look, sometimes you are stupid. Do you know what it's like out there? There is probably a safe word advertised in the Ladies loo if you are in trouble, or you ring me, get it?"

Joyce was a bit taken aback by what appeared sincere care, but it was too late for that now; she was on the way to a new life she told herself.

Joyce got the train from Fareham to Basingstoke - she could get from home to Fareham free on the bus. She sat on the train, almost alone in the carriage. Her emotions were very mixed, and as she had time now just staring out of the window, thoughts passed through her mind quicker than a horse running the Grand National.

She reflected on her last conversation with Hardy. It had been a bit of a reality check: she was not free of him, was she? She'd have to ring him, like a teenage girl checking in with parents. But then to be fair, that was not far from what she thought she ought to be doing, and what his response should have been. So why was she querying it? It was, she thought, because she should not have to respond to him at all and she resented it. This was top-line confusion.

And what was she going into this evening? Why had she put on sexy underwear when she had no intention of getting that close to the guy? And if she did, how was that going to work? Was he going to take her back to his place in Teddington?

She thought about getting out of the train at the next station and heading back to Fareham, but that would defeat everything she was trying to do. She realised that this was going to take some guts, as it was way outside her comfort zone.

The train arrived in Basingstoke all too soon. Although Charles said it was an easy walk from the station, Basingstoke seemed built for cars rather than pedestrians – there were roundabouts everywhere – so she took a taxi. She passed tall office blocks and flats on fast dual carriageways. Hardy would hate driving here, she told herself. Nowadays he couldn't handle anywhere if he didn't know which lane to get into, or anywhere where he didn't know where he was going. Then it hit her again: why on earth did Hardy come back into her mind? She must shake him off, she scolded herself.

She arrived about half an hour early. This was comfortable; she liked to be early for everything because it gave her a sense of control. She could choose where she sat and she had a good view of everything that was going on. She would also be composed and less flustered if she greeted him seated. She had a rough idea of what he looked like – how could she miss an ageing guy with very white teeth and jet-black hair?

She ordered a herbal tea, and true to form, chose a table

whereby she could observe everything. It was too early for the 'show crowd' and too late for those 'just visiting' who had probably long since left for their homes, so the place was almost empty. Only one table was occupied, with what looked like staff taking a break before the evening rush.

She had drunk her tea and it was now five-thirty, well past their 'about five' agreement. Joyce was nervous enough without being kept waiting. She vowed that she would only give him five minutes' grace, after which she would leave. She found herself almost hoping that he would not turn up … but he did.

He wore a black leather jacket, black jeans and a black T shirt and his long hair was grey rather than jet-black – and in a thin ponytail. But he was not unattractive, indeed to the point where she was pleasantly surprised.

He spotted her, and headed towards the table.

"Hello, you are Joyce?" his voice was gentle, just as it had been on the phone.

She stood, though was unsure why.

He leant into her, and did a continental greeting of a kiss on either cheek. This very act tensed Joyce. She didn't even like 'exchanging the sign of peace' with a fellow worshiper in church, let alone an act of affection when they had not even spoken yet. She was aware that she had suddenly become rigid.

"I hope you are Charles," she replied, which on reflection was a comical response, yet making the point that he could be anyone, and she was not in the habit of 'skin touching' so early in a relationship. In any case, his cheek and chin were rough; he had clearly not shaved to meet her.

Charles seemed unaware of the issues he presented: he was obviously a confident man.

"Can I get you a drink?" he asked straight away.

"No, I am fine thanks, I've only just finished this one."

"Do you mind if I go and get one for myself?"

"No, of course not, please do," she replied almost with relief.

His trip to the counter gave her time to think. Perhaps, she reasoned, he usually greeted people by kissing them; perhaps she was reading too much into it. Obviously, she told herself, he is an educated, sophisticated man, and more than likely such greeting gestures were normal for him.

Joyce studied his back, now he was facing the serving girl who had wrenched herself away from her colleagues still seated at their table. The leather jacket was well worn, the jeans did not hug his bottom, they hung, a little like a pair of curtains. He wore trainers which were slightly divorced from his jeans, enough to allow her to observe that he had trodden the heels right down. He definitely did not reek of money, she thought.

He arrived back with a coffee, and had bought himself a slice of carrot cake. She had not managed to spot his belly yet.

"Thank you for coming." he started. "Did you have a good journey?"

"Yes, thank you, it was entirely uneventful. Did you come by train?"

"No, I drove - it's quite easy to get out of Teddington and onto the M3. Only forty-five minutes or so by car."

Somewhere in the back of her mind, she seemed to recall that he had told her that he didn't drive. She decided, however, not to question it at this stage. In her mind, she checked out Teddington - that seemed fairly true, then. She found herself looking for lies all the time, and the one about not driving seemed like number one.

"Have you always lived in that area?"

"Oh God, no. I lived in Spain for years, and prior to that I lived in Devon. I was born in Hackney. So, what about you?" he asked. "Have you always lived in Gosport?"

"No, in fact we have only been there eight or nine years since my husband sold our business." Within seconds she realised that there was a lot wrong with that reply. At the very least she should have said 'ex-husband'. Not so much for Charles, more for her.

"Are you still both together?"

"No, of course not. I said 'we' because we did move to Gosport together, and of course it was 'our' business. No, we are separated now, we live apart."

He did not cross-question her.

"I paint, I paint more than I play, not really the right way round, but it keeps me busy. Have you seen my website?"

No she had not, but the production of his mobile meant that she was about to. She watched as he struggled to open various pages. Several of his fingernails were extraordinarily long.

"You need one of those prodder things for that," she ventured.

He ignored her, focused entirely on reaching the page that would show her his works.

"Oh," she said, and it took a few seconds to say anything else. Every single picture was – in Joyce's terms – erotic, verging on pornographic. His subjects were women of all ages, sometimes nude, sometimes draping stuff over themselves but still revealing the bits that Joyce thought should be covered.

"You obviously major in figure studies."

"Yes, I told you that on the phone. But I have done a couple of landscapes."

She had to admit that they were less interesting, even though he had managed to make even a tree look sexual.

"Any painter loves the shape of the female body," he said. "It is God-given at whatever age. Have you ever been painted?" He sounded very matter-of-fact.

She panicked a little – was this an invitation?

"No, I haven't, I don't even have many photographs of myself."

"Just about all of the women I paint find it exhilarating, or that's what they tell me. You should try it," he added.

"I don't think so." She was slightly annoyed at the forward nature of the man.

"Sorry, I've obviously annoyed you, and we have only been chatting two minutes – not doing very well, am I?"

"I am finding this difficult," she admitted. "I've got to admit that you are my first date in many years."

"Ah I see, yes, must be very difficult for you."

"Wasn't it difficult for you, when you first started dating again?"

"Not really, we had an open marriage and I chatted up women all the time, plus my work helped. It's an open ticket the minute you get the clothes off a woman."

Joyce was beginning to think she was out of her depth here. She had heard of 'open' marriages, but only by reading about them in the tabloids or in women's magazines.

"Well, Charles, you have a lot of advantages over me. My life seems to have been very boring compared to yours. So, if you were in an open marriage, what actually broke you two up?" She congratulated herself on such a probing question and he seemed taken aback, not answering straight away.

"My wife, Debbie, has some strange ways. Lots of artistic people do, and let's just say they were not compatible with mine. Can we leave it at that for the moment?"

"Of course. It just seemed strange to me that such a liberal arrangement could have anything embedded in it that could destroy a marriage." She didn't want to leave it there, of course: she was now desperate to find out what had happened to them.

"Well, as I said, it's all a bit complicated to go into here. So, you have no kids? What about other relatives?"

"None on either side."

"Cheap Christmas then," he said, jokingly.

"Yes, I suppose it is. Also a lonely one compared to all the family fun they portray on TV programmes."

They seemed to be going round in circles, both asking questions, but neither listening to the other. Suddenly, without warning, Charles stood and waved wildly at the window. Joyce wondered what on earth was going on, and turning round in the now dulling light she spotted a blonde woman alighting from an old Renault. She was engaged in taking something out of the car and was not looking round at that moment.

"It's Debbie!" he said. He had become very animated and almost excited.

This was obviously 'the' big event, or so it felt that way to Joyce. She had noticed Charles had been preoccupied, constantly looking out of the window – now she understood why.

"Oh, is she joining us?" asked Joyce, somewhat bemused.

He didn't answer but took several steps away from the table and towards a window closer to where the car was parked. he continued the extraordinary windmill-like waving of his arms. Debbie, Joyce noted, was still furrowing around in the car, bent over rather exposing the shape of her rear end in her black tight skirt. Why wave when he can see she is not looking, Joyce wondered? He then started calling out frantically.

"Debs! Debs! Debs!"

"I would be surprised if she can hear you through this glass. Why don't you go out and get her?"

Charles seemed oblivious to anything Joyce was saying, who by now was beginning to think this was verging on being rude to her. But he rescued it just in time. He turned to her.

"It's Debbie!" Charles was excited, and Joyce somewhat annoyed. Was this how dating worked these days?

"Oh, you don't say! I would never have guessed." Oh, that's more like it, the bitch coming out in me now, she thought. However, the remark appeared to have gone right over Charles's head.

Debbie eventually stood up from the driver's door, clutching a bag and some other parcel, a box, a brown box with what looked like a plant protruding from it.

"Oh Christ!" exclaimed Charles and with that he ran from the cafe out to the car park.

By now Debs had put the box and bag on the bonnet, while she took the key from the ignition to lock the car. Charles got to her just as she resumed an upright position. The ritual greeting was identical to that which had been offered to Joyce. Charles leant immediately in towards her and kissed her on both cheeks. Debs was obviously much more used to this greeting than Joyce, and responded by putting an affectionate arm around his neck and shoulders.

They exchanged a few words, which Joyce could not

hear, but she saw Charles point towards the box then grab it. He seemed anxious, and left carrying the box in front of him like a tray. He walked at speed while she just stood there staring at him. Joyce continued to watch as he placed the box in the boot of what she assumed was his car. He hurried back to Debbie, grabbed her arm and marched her towards the door of the cafe.

When they came in together, he no longer had her by the arm. Joyce was finding this both bewildering and amusing. Debbie had shoulder-length blonde hair and must have been in her mid-forties, Joyce guessed. She looked both slim and shapely, but it was difficult to tell under her winter clothing. She was only slightly shorter that Charles, and to be quite blunt, Joyce felt they looked an ideal couple. There was a certain engagement there which Joyce felt unnerving.

"This is my ex-wife, Debbie," Charles announced. Debbie proffered a hand towards Joyce

"And this is Joyce. Joyce comes from Gosport."

"Oh hello … er, where's that?" asked Debbie.

Joyce could not place Debbie's accent; she thought she could hear some Australian in there, but then it might be central America.

"It's a part of Portsmouth," Charles informed her.

"No it's not," said Joyce. "It is opposite Portsmouth on the harbour entrance, but is certainly is not part of Portsmouth."

"Ah, obviously a sore point," said Charles.

"You could say so – we get fed up with being called Portsmouth on the telly."

Debbie pulled a seat out to sit on, while Charles offered to get her a coffee, leaving the two women uncomfortably alone with each other. Joyce wondered what you say to someone that you meet on a first date with her ex.

"So you are performing tonight then?" Joyce eventually broke the uneasy silence.

"I am indeed. But hey, I'm going to say it even if you are not - what is that arsehole playing at here?" She seemed furious.

Joyce felt relieved. At least 'Debs' had walked into this as well as her.

"He is sometimes so thick," said Debbie, "and he is totally unaware of people's feelings. I think sometimes he is a little bit mad, mental – you know?"

"Well, I am beginning to think that myself." Joyce replied.

"OMG," she said, "oh, that is bad of me. I shouldn't really be running him down to you on his first date. He is a very talented man, he has lots of good points – he is loyal, a great friend and well …. I'll leave it there for the moment."

Joyce was intrigued as to what other less favourable qualities Debbie might have named, but had no chance to challenge her as Charles returned bearing Debbie's coffee.

"Sorry, that was a bit rude of me, Joyce, I didn't ask you if you wanted anything."

"No thanks, I am fine. Are we eating at all tonight?" Joyce asked tentatively

"No." Nothing else, just 'no'.

That was clear then.

"I need to eat something." Joyce said. "I haven't had anything since breakfast."

"He doesn't eat until really late, gone eleven most nights," Debbie informed Joyce.

"Well, I'm sorry, that's no good for me. I wouldn't be able to sleep, it would all repeat on me if you know what I mean. I need something now."

"I'll see what they have here," said Charles. "Would you

like a sandwich if they do one?"

This guy was beginning to make Hardy look a real smoothie. He seemed to have no regard at all that he was supposed to be on a date with Joyce.

"I think she was hoping for a something a bit more substantial, Charles." Debbie was really helping out here, but then she obviously knew him better than anyone. "Just go and see what they can do for her."

He obeyed; he seemed to do whatever she told him, almost like a mother-child relationship.

Debbie took the opportunity to confide in Joyce.

"You're probably thinking that his behaviour is a little odd. The truth is that he has been diagnosed as being on the autistic spectrum. He is quite unable to understand any emotion whatsoever and incapable of empathy. It's not his fault – he can do little about it – but to be frank, it's hell to live with. He will say all the right things; he does this by what is called 'learnt behaviour', so yes, he will tell you he loves you because that's what he believes is the right thing to say, especially when he is having sex with you."

Joyce was both intrigued and suspicious. Was this ex-wife trying to warn against a relationship that she did not want her ex to have? However, the revelation of Charles' autism didn't really surprise Joyce, in the short time she had known him, it explained his not-quite-right behaviour.

"He has actually been diagnosed, has he?" Joyce asked eventually.

"Yes, we went to marriage guidance several years ago, and they first suggested he might have autism. But I think it's got worse as he's got older. Yet on the other hand he has got better at hiding it, especially since the diagnosis."

"I never picked up anything when I was speaking to him on the phone, and arranging this 'date'. I have to say, though, that I certainly didn't think when I set out this morning that I would be sitting with his ex-wife talking in such terms."

"I had no idea he was going to meet someone on a date, he only told me in the car park just now."

"Unbelievable," Joyce proffered. "With his autism," she continued, "does he get violent?" Joyce had decided to ask outright: even at this stage it was an important question. "I've heard that some people with autism need a physical outlet for their frustration."

"It's difficult to say, because we did some stuff early on in our marriage that seemed to please him but that did involve some – shall we say – rough stuff."

Joyce had by now heard enough. Having got out of one relationship, which on reflection seemed almost boring, did she really want to get into something this complicated? She felt mentally worn out after just twenty minutes here. Without further ado, she put her coat on.

"Give him my apologies, Debbie, I'm afraid I am out of this, I don't need this sort of hassle at my time of life."

"Oh no – I shouldn't have said what I said. You should find these things out for yourself and make your own judgement."

"You've saved me the bother and frankly, Debbie, I am grateful. No harm has been done so let's just move on and away."

"Phew!" said Joyce as she took her seat on the train. That was one hell of a date! If this was the world of online dating, then she was not enamoured of it. Hardy was bound to ask her how things went, and why she was back home so early. "Oh God!" she said out loud.

Hardy had not crowed. He did not need to. In fact he cooked her some eggs and bacon while she was changing. He did not question her about her date and that, in a peculiar sort of way, irritated her. Why did he never seem to care? He went back upstairs, and shortly she heard the normal drone of the telly. Back to boring normal then.

"Surely there must be ordinary men out there," she said to herself. She was not prepared to give up on the dating sites after just one experience. She re-visited her tablet, which she noted was now looking grubby where her hand constantly held it. To her surprise she had a message waiting for her on the dating site.

His name was Roger. He was 68 and was a retired Naval Officer. His previous wife had 'passed on', he said, a year ago. This seemed more promising. On top of that, he lived in Portsmouth: almost too good to be true. Joyce swiped right, and all seemed well. His email allowed her to send a message so she sent one straight away: a bland message describing herself as a normal woman. No email returned but instead the website informed her the 'client' was no longer active. Always the same, she thought: anything that looks any good is no longer active.

CHAPTER SEVEN
A Visit from the Police

It was three weeks later when Hardy answered the door to two policemen who wanted to speak to Joyce.

"Hang on, I'll check if she's in." He shouted down the hallway: "Joyce, Joyce – it's for you."

"I'm in the toilet. Who is it?"

"Police."

"What?"

"Police."

"Oh gawd, just a minute. What do they want?" she shouted through the closed door of the toilet.

"She asked what you want?"

"May I ask who you are, sir?" asked the policeman quite pleasantly.

"I'm her husband." Hardy's thoughts went immediately as to whether he should elaborate on that, but in the same millisecond decided it was too difficult.

"We would like to speak to her privately, sir, if you don't mind." replied the policeman.

"Well you heard, she's in the toilet at the moment."

"Yes sir, we can wait."

"Do you want to come in and wait in here?"

"Thank you."

This was suddenly difficult. The house was upside down due to the bizarre arrangements. Joyce had washing drying on a clothes horse.

She eventually appeared.

"Oh hello," she said.

"I'll go upstairs then." Hardy withdrew from the scene, but of course not from earshot.

"Good morning ma'm. Am I speaking to Joyce?" She nodded.

"Can you confirm your surname for us please?" Joyce confirmed her surname, now with some concern. "Joyce, I won't beat about the bush. Your name appeared on a chat within a dating site, and we have good reason to believe that you dated a man named Charles, who we believe to be Charles Bowyer, or one of the other aliases he uses."

Joyce frowned, both bewildered and a little bit worried. She decided to be upfront. She had nothing to hide.

"Yes, I met a man called Charles in Basingstoke ... must have been a couple of weeks ago now."

The policeman was accompanied by a policewoman, who now spoke.

"Would that have been Saturday 3rd of November?"

"Yes, it probably was, can't swear to the date."

"Can you tell us exactly what happened at this meeting?" the policeman asked.

"Sorry, what are you looking for? I mean it was a very strange meeting but then I haven't done this sort of thing before, you understand. Do you mind if we keep our voices down?"

"Would you rather do this somewhere else?" the policewoman asked.

"Oh no, here is fine but look, my husband and I live separately. You may find this odd but we have decided to live our own lives. So I am not 'cheating' on him as such because, you know, I am a free agent so to speak. I don't want you to get the wrong impression, yet at the same time I don't particularly want him earwigging at the top of the stairs." Joyce's explanation was showing a certain amount of nervousness and self-consciousness.

The officers did not bat an eyelid. Joyce supposed they had come across all sorts of scenarios in their time.

"You said, Joyce, that you found it a very strange meeting. Can you elaborate on that?"

"Well for one thing, his ex-wife turned up. I mean, I was meant to be watching her perform on stage later that evening, but I never ever expected her to join us."

"How did she join you? Did she just walk in?" the policeman asked.

"No, and that was what was a bit peculiar. Charles saw her car arrive and started calling to her through the window of the cafe, like he was calling a dog. Then he rushed out to her and greeted her as if they were still good friends. It made me very wary, I can tell you." Joyce was beginning to get on her high horse.

"Was there anything else you noticed when he was greeting her?" the policeman asked.

"Not really. She gave him a box or something and he ran with it over to his car, or I assumed it was his car."

"Did it appear heavy?"

"Not particularly, because he was able to run with it, but it had something sticking out the top."

"Did you see what it was?"

"Not really, it was getting dusk at that point."

"Right, thank you Joyce, thank you very much. Look, your personal circumstances are nothing to do with us, who you meet and that sort of thing is not illegal, and you have done nothing wrong. It's just that you may have witnessed the aftermath of a criminal transaction, and we may need you to make a statement, or appear in court for us."

Joyce had always seen herself as a public-spirited citizen. She had little time for all these people who refused to help the police based on fear or intimidation. Now it seemed she might have to do her duty.

"Oh, my goodness. Can I ask what he has been doing?"

"Not him, her. What name did she use with you.?"

"Debbie."

"Right, that's just one of many names she uses."

"Well I am astounded. I have to ask, where would I have come into this?"

"We suspect you would have been used as a courier had you not left when you did."

"A courier?"

"Yes, the parcel contained controlled drugs and a consignment of cash."

"You are joking." Joyce was taken aback.

"No, there's no better cover than a lovely little old lady transporting drugs. You would turn out to be one of their 'county lines'. A 'mule' in fact."

Little old lady! She fumed inside.

"The fact that you saw the transfer of the box from her to him helps us enormously."

She agreed, even though she was not quite sure of what she was agreeing to. What she was sure of was that if she embarked on an online date again, she should take things considerably more slowly.

With that, the police were gone, leaving Joyce behind them. She started to cry, which immediately brought Hardy downstairs.

"Joyce, are you alright?"

"I will be shortly."

"Is there anything I can do?" Hardy asked, genuinely.

"No, not really, they just want me to give evidence about something I witnessed."

"An accident or something?" Hardy probed.

She stopped crying, aware suddenly she was being cross-questioned yet again, and that his motive was probably not to comfort her. She did, however, decide to be open with him, which served two purposes, to show him that she was moving on and to pre-empt him seeing any reports in the papers or on the news.

"So, you were to be an ox then?" he said, more a statement than a question. Joyce looked at him blankly. "You know, someone who transports drugs for others."

It dawned on her.

"No, that's a mule, you stupid man."

They both saw the funny side of that, and joined each other in laughing.

It was several days later when Joyce was asked to provide a written statement.

The year was pushing towards Christmas now, and things started to feel not right for both of them. They were still attending church services and 'do's' together, quite unable to go public with their bizarre lifestyle.

Joyce vowed to do something about this, because she felt unable to make new friends, and had ruled out another try at online dating for the time being.

Her first experience had been enough to satisfy her curiosity, although she still dabbled on the site and 'chatted', but never took matters further. Perhaps she could just hint to their friends, let them make their own minds up.

The vicar's after-service sherry party was the ideal venue, surrounded as she was by the inner core of parishioners, the reliable group, the commandos even. It had been here a year ago that the seeds of their protest idea had flourished, and that six of them had embarked upon. Alas, there was only five now with the tragic death of Bert, her little fat round friend.

Here she could drop hints, over the disgusting sherry.

Ken enquired as to their health, a natural thing to do in a social setting like that.

"Well it's not all roses," Joyce replied.

Unfortunately for Joyce, Ken knew her too well to delve deeper into that, preferring to keep things general.

"They reckon there is some new virus coming from China." Ken moved the conversation on.

Joyce found that she listened to news less and less since she and Hardy were living 'apart', and she had not heard anything about it.

"Long way away – doubt it will get here," she replied.

She was doing her best to look 'separated' from Hardy, but was aware no one in the room was taking any notice. Their behaviour as a couple was well known, and today was little different to any other time they appeared in public.

Hardy was deep in conversation with Olly, his 'right hand man', as Hardy called him. In Joyce's eyes, it was more the other way around. The protest on the Gosport Ferry had more than exposed Hardy's inadequacies, particularly when he had a few drinks. It had been the nail in the coffin of their relationship, their 'Road to Damascus' moment.

She felt the need to leave: she did not want to be in the same room living this lie.

"Right, I need to get going," she announced.

No one took much notice, except to say the odd goodbye, and the vicar 'blessed' her. Hardy ignored her and carried on his conversation.

Olly's wife rushed over, proffering a card for her. It was addressed to both her and Hardy, yet even now all Joyce could say was "Oh thank you." She felt a sense of panic; she was feeling hot, edgy and almost on the verge of breaking down in public. It had come on in seconds: she had to go.

"Is she alright?" Olly asked Hardy.

"Don't know, she does have some funny turns lately. We try to keep out of each other's way at home you know."

"That's got to be difficult."

"Well, not if you arrange things properly. I still see her and chat occasionally, but not that often."

"Sorry, I did not mean to probe – personal relations are not my thing, as you probably know."

But it was enough. His wife had picked it up and later that day ran with it. Olly hardly had a clue as to what she was on about.

"Oh come on, Olly, they are living apart, I am telling you, and when I mentioned it to Sarah she agreed with me."

"Well she would, wouldn't she? There's nothing more juicy for you women than relationship ups-and-downs."

"Mark my words, Olly, there are big problems there this time."

Joyce poured herself a glass of wine when she got home, and was almost relieved when she heard the front door open some quarter of an hour later.

"Is that you Hardy?" she called.

"Yeah, are you alright?"

"Not really, I came over quite peculiar in that room."

"It didn't go unnoticed. How are you feeling now?"

"Seem to be OK now. I just had a glass of wine." She pointed to the now empty glass.

"Blimey, that's unusual for you."

"I think I should have had it before we went to church really, I needed some Dutch courage and that awful stuff the vicar serves up doesn't help."

"Why did you need Dutch courage?"

"Well I was going to tell people that we are living apart – I can't keep this public lie going."

"Well I did mention it to Olly and his wife," Hardy mumbled.

"You what? You mentioned it?"

"I told them we didn't see much of each other in the house."

"Good God, you actually told them that? Why?"

"Thought it was the right thing to do." Hardy was slightly on the defensive now.

"Well I was going to tell them today, but it just didn't happen, did it?"

"Not my fault. Anyway, what do you reckon was wrong with you? Did you feel faint or what?"

"I think it was a panic attack. I was worrying too much about telling them about us. Just got to the point where I had to escape, get air, if you know what I mean."

CHAPTER EIGHT

Milk Straight from the Cow

Joyce had not entirely given up 'looking for love' online. She was aware that these sites had the ability to become addictive. She would keep visiting them more for amusement, she told herself, than for anything else. But …

His name was Morris; Morris de Minorie. What a classic name she thought to herself. The photo was neither attractive nor unattractive. His hair had seen better days, but that could be said of just about all candidates suitable for her affection. His profile was more encouraging: it said he was a farmer, who owned his own farm. It was primarily beef, and he bred a breed called Dexters. His farm was in the Meon Valley, which was not far – though might as well have been a thousand miles away when she didn't have a car.

Joyce decided to do a 'like'. She was returned with a 'like' within minutes, hence a chat started.

'I see you are a beef farmer,' Joyce typed.

'Yes.'

'You must be busy?'

'Yes.'

It had been barely a minute, and already Joyce was beginning to think that this was going to be hard work. One more attempt:

'Do you live alone? I mean do you have help?'

'Just me, but I have a brother and his wife who help every so often.'

Ah, that's a bit better, she thought. Perhaps she should wait and see if he came back with any questions for her. But a farmer, she thought, would be quite a catch – an interesting life … and plenty of cash.

'Do you know anything about farming?' he asked eventually.

'Not a thing, so you would have plenty to teach me.'

Was that a bit forward she wondered? But that's what this internet stuff does to you.

'Would you like me to show you around?'

That was a bit quick, Joyce thought, but then she in turn had been a bit forward; she had really walked into that one. What would be the harm anyway? She could go to Fareham by bus and he could pick her up from there.

They duly arranged the date: he would pick her up on Saturday morning. But already there were definitions to sort out – simple things like what was 'early' for him was the middle of the night for Joyce. They decided on 10.15am. Joyce had remembered that she couldn't use her bus pass until half past nine, and she certainly had no intention of paying for the journey.

Joyce crossed to West Street from the bus station. Morris had told her he would wait in his Land Rover. There was one parked roughly where he said it would be, but she didn't think this could possibly belong to a 'gentleman farmer'. It was the traditional old green colour and was covered in mud splatters. It had a pale green canvas covering the rear, ripped in several places. The door to this vehicle suddenly opened, and out stepped a man who slightly resembled the image in the photo.

Either his hair was greasy or he had plastered it in hair cream, a substance not used these days even by Hardy. Looking at the rest of him, Joyce decided it probably was grease. If he had dressed for the occasion, then he certainly had failed. He still had wellie boots on. His trousers were dark green, with patches of something on them., and tucked into wellington boots. His jumper had a hole in the right elbow.

"How do? You must be Joyce."

This was initially a disappointment. She had been expecting a man in cords, a smart shirt and perhaps a tweed jacket.

"I'm sorry, I 'ad no time to change, 'ad a problem with an 'effer this morn."

Joyce had little idea of what Morris was talking about. He fitted the image of a farmer when talking, or rather mumbling. She had to make a decision as to whether or not to get into the Land Rover. Her inclination was not to, yet part of her said that if she'd come this far, she should at least give it a go.

The seat had been used an awful lot. The floor was bare metal that someone had painted blue. The doors were basic with no padding and a metal handle. The windows slid on gliders, which had gone green with moss. At least he couldn't lock her in, she thought. The seat belt went round her stomach, not over her shoulder, and she fretted as to whether this was legal. Morris had by now circumnavigated the vehicle, and was getting into the driving seat.

"That is a huge steering wheel," Joyce observed.

"'Spose it is. Don't get 'em like this anymore."

He inserted the key. The engine seemed to wind up rather than just start. It was unbelievably noisy and clearly conversation was going to be impossible during the journey. The gearbox crashed into first gear and they jumped forward. A horn sounded; Morris had obviously annoyed the BMW driver behind him by pulling out without looking. It seemed to have no effect on Morris whatsoever that the male driver was gesticulating and mouthing obscenities at him.

"He'll be alright later," was Morris's response.

But of course, the BMW driver had to wait a lot longer to be alright, now stuck behind Morris, who was doing a maximum speed of forty-five mph. At that speed, the odd speck of mud was released from his rear tyres.

The 'Landy' plodded up the A32 slowly and noisily. It seemed to wander, not always going where Morris aimed. There was little conversation due to the noise of the engine, but Joyce asked what was in retrospect the wrong question. It did open Morris up, however.

"So this is quite old, Morris," said Joyce meaning the Land Rover.

"Yeah, I've had it for about four years, picked it up from a Ministry sale. It had come back from RAF Akrotiri in Cyprus. It's a series 2A and from the early sixties, I think."

This reminded Joyce of Hardy, the smell of hot oil, the sounds of grinding gears, and the ever-moving steering wheel. And then she saw Morris's hands, thick and powerful, with fingers like sausages, but more than that – grimy.

The ride lasted about forty minutes. They had turned off to the left somewhere she did not recognise. The lane narrowed and became muddy. Farm gates went by and a house appeared through one of them. They turned into a yard that could only be described as dilapidated. Joyce was somewhat apprehensive about going into the house, and indeed this was breaking all the rules about going into someone's house on a first date.

Her apprehension was well placed. A dirty sheepdog ran to greet them. It jumped up at Morris, wet and muddy. Joyce's worst fears were realised when it turned its attentions to her. Morris didn't seem to understand that such affection from such a dirty filthy lump of hairy dog was unwelcome.

"Please stop it before it jumps up at me," she begged

"'E won't hurt you."

"Maybe not, but I don't want him making my clothes dirty."

That seemed to make more sense to Morris. The front door was open, and they walked into the flagstoned hall. The place had seen no fresh paint in years. The hall was a vaguely brown colour, which Joyce assumed had once been white or cream. They passed a door which Joyce assumed went to a lounge, and headed to the kitchen.

Joyce wanted to leave, but this was not up to her. She would have to ask Morris and she didn't even know the address. What was the name of this farm? She was beginning to panic. She had her mobile and was forming an action plan. If the worst came to the worst she would run out of the gate, get herself clear and ring Hardy or the police. The idea comforted her temporarily.

"'Spec you'd like a cup of tea?"

There was a range, black with chrome lids over the cooking surfaces. A black kettle that looked like it held half a gallon was perched on one side.

"Won't take two mins to boil, keeps warm on the top there all the time."

"Thank you." That was all Joyce could say.

"Milk and sugar?"

"Oh, just milk please."

Morris got a stainless-steel jug out of a fridge and told her it was milk fresh from a cow that morning. He made the tea in a pot, but with just one spoon of tea. Frugal, she thought.

"So, have you lived here long?" Joyce eventually asked while the tea was brewing.

"All me life. Mum and Dad both died here. I still feel dear mum, you know. She rested on that very table before they took her off for burial. I can still see 'er now."

The 'very' table was the one Joyce now leant on, which she found herself suddenly recoiling from.

"Was very sad. My brother had fallen out with 'er, and she left the whole farm to me. 'E turned on me at the wake, you know. Not my fault I said, it was you who fell out with 'er, I had nothing to do with it. Still didn't stop 'im landing a right-hander on me in the middle of the pub. Silly, that was. Everyone in the pub turned on 'im and 'e went off in a huff. It was not the time nor the place, see?"

"Of course, that sort of thing should have waited. Perhaps when you were both alone."

"Well, haven't spoke to 'im since." Morris said.

"That's so so sad. How long has this been going on?"

"Oh a while, must be the week before last," Morris replied.

"Oh, that long." Joyce had expected him to say years. That meant his mother had been lying dead on this very table only days ago. It made her feel a little weird.

The tea was hot and steamy but looked grey. Joyce was more accustomed to a browny colour. It tasted weak due to the amount of milk he'd poured in and it had a sickly taste.

They sat around the table.

"So there you are then, I own all this."

Joyce was wondering whether he was trying to tell her that he was very wealthy, and that she would be a fool to ignore him. But somehow, all the money in the world would not tempt Joyce into this filthy hole. She was, however, prepared not to be rude at the moment because Morris's behaviour was not offensive in any way. He was just hard work to converse with, and obviously not used to interacting with people, let alone a woman on a date. In fact, she thought, he was more genuine than lots of men who kept going on about themselves.

"Do you want to look around?" Morris eventually proffered.

"Thank you, but I don't think I'm really dressed for it. I hadn't expected to be invited to look over a farm, I thought maybe you were taking us to lunch."

"Oh." The conversation died again. Morris had no response to that. And he didn't seem bothered that he had no response.

Joyce was still struggling through her tea. The richness of the milk was new to her and its sickly smell. She took another sip. Then it suddenly got worse. Tea leaves! A mouthful of tea leaves. This had not happened in years. The revulsion must have shown on her face.

"Sorry about the tea leaves, I ain't got a strainer. Mother must have put it away and I can't find it."

"I need some water,' croaked Joyce.

The water was forthcoming, and she ran to the sink to wash her mouth free from the offending leaves. This was not turning out to be an ideal date, and Joyce was beginning to wonder whether such a thing existed.

Morris seemed bewildered, almost as if he had shut

down completely. He suddenly said, without explanation:

"I'll take you back to Fareham, then."

For all her reservations, the remark still took Joyce by surprise. She felt a sense of relief but also a sense that she had not treated this man with enough respect.

"Well, I think that would probably be best, don't you?" she admitted.

It was now almost lunchtime and she wondered if she should suggest they stop at a pub on the way back, but decided it was best just to get it over with.

"I need to change," said Morris. "I need to go to the bank when I get to Fareham, so I'll take the car."

'So the Land Rover was not his only form of transport? When Morris disappeared into what Joyce assumed was his bedroom, she had a look around the kitchen. The place was filthy, there was no getting away from that. Two cats had come in and were now carrying out ablutions on the draining board. They looked very much at home.

Against one wall was a fashionably distressed Welsh dresser, with mugs hung from hooks. The dressed rocked because the flagstone floor was uneven and Joyce realised the 'distressing' was probably from years of use. She wondered what scenes this kitchen had witnessed over the many years. She lurched between feeling sorry for Morris and wanting to get out of this situation as fast as she could. She also reasoned that 'feeling sorry' was no basis for a relationship.

Morris re-appeared, looking quite presentable. He had added a tie to his old shirt but was still wearing an ancient and stained cap.

"We'll take the other car I 'spose," he said. What emerged from behind a pile of hay bales was a brand new, enormous Range Rover. This time she was to be treated to leather seats, heating and no smells other than that subtle scent of new car.

Joyce couldn't resist asking: "Why did you pick me up in that old Land Rover when you could have given me a nicer impression in this?"

"Ahh, well you see, I know lots of women just want men with money. I always think if you are not a gold digger, then you would have no problem with the Landy."

"How bizarre!" Joyce exclaimed.

"I know about that sort of thing. Just after me money and land," Morris countered.

Joyce assumed her insulted stance, her head rising straight, her eyes piercing and her hands on her hips. The gesture was lost on Morris. He opened the door for Joyce and she climbed in.

The journey back was much more comfortable and Morris seemed to relax now he was 'getting rid of her'.

"I went out with the AI girl last week, but she don't want to go again."

"AI girl?" Joyce was bewildered.

"Oh, course, 'spose you don't know what that is."

"No, I don't."

There was silence.

"Well are you going to tell me?"

"You might not like it."

"What do you mean I might not like it?" She was getting annoyed again.

"Well, it means 'artificial insemination'. She transfers sperm from bulls to heifers in a sort of pump jobby."

Joyce understood now.

"So why doesn't she want to go out with you again?"

"Said I was a tight-fisted bastard."

"Good lord, that was frank. Whatever did you do to earn

such an accolade?"

"Acco what?"

"Sorry I was being sarcastic. Why did she call you that? I mean, did you not take her out for a meal or anything?"

"Yeah, I took her out to eat – mind you, it was a bit cold."

"A bit cold?"

"There was a bit of a wind blowing, and of course sat up on Portsdown Hill, well it's cold up there at the best of times."

"You sat out on Portsdown Hill?"

"Yeah, it's nice up there, looks out all over Portsmouth."

Joyce was well aware that the views were indeed outstanding, but hardly the sort of place you take a woman on a first date.

"Don't tell me you bought her a burger from that guy who trades in that little car park?"

"Oh God, no!"

"So you took her to the pub?" This was not easy, Joyce thought.

"No. I'd made some really nice sandwiches, with my own butter but she said they smelt of sick."

Joyce said nothing, but 'tight bastard' really did go through her mind. She did still feel sorry for him, though – he was never going to get anywhere with a member of the opposite sex. Perhaps he had never had a role model?

She was aware that she was in danger of volunteering. That was not the aim, it would do her no good and get her in deep where she did not want to even paddle.

"But look, Morris, that's not what's expected when you take a girl out on a date. They expect to be wooed, made to feel special, not given a sandwich to munch in the car."

"No, I'm starting to believe that, but then on the other hand I don't want to be seen as a guy that is an easy take."

"Of course you don't." Joyce realised he was beyond help. As she got out of the car, she felt an enormous sense of relief. There was also embarrassment: Morris had driven right into the bus station, looking for a bus that was about to leave for Gosport. He parked behind a Number Two, completely blocking its ability to reverse out. He checked Joyce was safely seated on the bus before he drove off, with the bus-driver getting out to wave his fist and shout after him. Morris seemed oblivious.

The driver got back on board.

"Do you know that man?" he said to Joyce, his face still angry.

"No."

"But you got out of his car."

"I may have got out of his car, but I can assure you that today is the first day I have ever met him, and I can assure you it will be the last as well."

CHAPTER NINE

A Woman from Cologne

Hardy had reservations about this one: she was seventy-one but her picture seemed to indicate that she was a lot younger than that. He figured it was an old photo, recycled numerous times.

He was to meet her in a nice Italian restaurant in Fareham, quite easy really, and one where he could catch a bus using his pensioner bus pass. No costs there, and it also allowed him to have a drink if he wanted.

She was already there when he arrived, and bore a startling resemblance to her photograph. He decided not to be so cynical about everyone he contacted. She was almost still blonde, long hair done in a bun at the back, with only a few shades of grey. She had glasses perched on the end of her nose, while nervously perusing the menu. The menu was obviously providing defence from the half-occupied restaurant, and she seemed relieved to see this old crock of a guy come towards her. "Hello, I hope you are Ushi?" He congratulated himself for that line, which sounded quite smooth, he thought.

"Yes, I am, and you must be Hardy."

"Pleased to meet you, and may I say you look identical to your photograph online."

"Why wouldn't I?" she asked almost aggressively, giving him a strange look.

"Oh sorry, I didn't mean it rudely. May I sit?"

"Of course." she said, almost conciliatory.

"I hope I'm not late."

"No, you're on time, I always like to be early for everything. I'm the sort of person who spends hours in cafes in airport lounges because I'm so early for a flight." She smiled. Hardy took it that that was meant to be amusing.

"Oh, early is always better than being late," he said, a neutral response that had the effect of closing down the conversation. This was another one which was going to be hard work, he thought.

"So, Hardy, you are divorced?"

"Separated." He felt it was only a partial lie. "And you?"

"My husband is late."

"Late? Late for what?" Hardy was a bit bewildered.

"Late. Dead. Do you not say when a person has died that they are 'late', like the late Terry Wogan?"

It dawned on him, but he thought it a peculiar use of the language.

"I must point out," she continued, "that I was born in Germany and still find the nuances of the English language difficult to follow."

"Well, you're not alone there – lots of English people have difficulty with the language. "When did you come over here?"

"As a child, but I went back for years with my husband."

"That must have been hard as a child in a foreign country?"

"My German mother came here as the wife of a British soldier. He was clearing up the mess of Cologne."

Hardy was suddenly really interested. He liked history, especially when it was first-hand.

It was Hardy's turn this time not to have looked at the menu when the waitress came over. However, unlike Edna, he could decide in seconds: it was going to be lasagne and a good red. But that was an interruption and he was eager to hear more.

"Go on then, tell me about those early days," he said. "How did your parents meet?"

"Well, Cologne was in ruins. The saving grace was that the cathedral – the Döm – was largely intact, with only shrapnel damage from bombs that had been aimed at the bahnhof, and the bridges over the Rhine. It was not much consolation to Ursula, a young blonde girl who had returned to the city to find her brother, now demobbed from the Wehrmacht. Of course, that girl was to be my mother."

"Had most of the family survived the bombing?"

"Yes – her brother Horst had survived, so had his wife and sister. But her father – my grandfather – had committed suicide because he had been a high-ranking policeman under the Hitler regime. Death seemed preferable to being caught by the Russians. Everyone was frightened of the Russians, with their reputation for brutality. But all Horst's money was gone, he had no job and there was chaos in the streets with little food."

"Were the Allies helping by this time?" asked Hardy.

"Yes, and Cologne was a priority because it was a strategic crossing of the Rhine. Jobs started to appear, but only for those who had not been sympathetic to the Nazis. My mother had been employed by the Wehrmacht as private secretary to various ranking officers, so the Allies regarded her with suspicion. She did get a job, though – and that's how she met my father."

Ushi took a sip of her wine.

"It was the day that news had come through about the dropping of a H-bomb on Japan. She was out looking for work when she spotted a very handsome British soldier.

He was clearly an officer, but his uniform was dishevelled, his boots unbrushed, and he wore his peaked cap cocked. My mother was immediately drawn to him. He was smoking and talking to some men who were armed with nothing more than shovels. Ursula looked good, she knew that. Her clothes were better than most, having been bought for her in fashionable Berlin in the early years of the war. She wore a fur coat, had her hair piled high and was wearing high heels.

"The officer smiled at her and asked if she was looking for work – he said he wanted a PA to do translation work and asked whether she could speak English as well as German. She told him she could, but that she wasn't approved. He had no truck with that and told her to turn up at the barracks the next morning and ask for Major Alan Wadey."

"And presumably it wasn't just a job he was offering?"

"Exactly. I was born in 1946. Of course, I don't remember much about Germany, but when we relocated to England, I was apparently a right mess due to malnutrition. My father ditched my mother almost immediately. I remember we travelled from house to house where she was a live-in housekeeper and often we would be subject to abuse because we were German. Eventually, she settled down with a man who turned out to be a friend of Alan's. They paid for me to go to a convent school, and even there, some of the teachers were hostile to me. But that is how it was in those days: since then, life has turned out not to be too bad at all."

She had hardly paused to draw breath, and whilst Hardy found it interesting he put the non-stop monologue down to nervousness, She hadn't finished, however.

"I got married very young," she said. "Maybe I felt better with an English surname, maybe also I felt more secure because I married into a huge family who embraced me and made me feel part of them. We divorced about five years ago, but of course we have a daughter between us, so I still saw him every so often."

"You tell the story so well." said Hardy, genuinely impressed. Every so often, he could hear a slight German accent, but one had to listen very hard to find it.

"The UK has been good to me, and it's a real shame that our countries are no longer working together, now that the UK has left the EU."

Hardy wondered whether he should comment, whether this was some sort of 'test' to probe his political views, but he was not given time to respond.

She continued: "My husband died a year ago. I am now fully mourned and ready to meet other men."

This was said in a very matter of fact way, almost as if she had rehearsed it. She continued in much the same vein, as if she was laying down ground rules.

"I miss male company," she said. "I miss the excitement that a man brings to a relationship. I have fantasies, you know?"

Hardy felt this was far too much intimate information for a first date. Was he supposed to ask what these fantasies were? Were all women so upfront about their 'needs' these days? He was beginning to think so. It also went through his mind that all the women he had met were more exciting than Joyce, but perhaps it was the novelty.

"Men are so contrary but so needed by many of us women," she said. Hardy felt she was delivering a lecture. "My husband was a real gentleman until it came to sex, when he became a lover of considerable capacity and strength."

Hardy almost choked on his lasagne. He felt so uncomfortable, but on the other hand, this was the sort of exciting conversation he had been seeking.

"I doubt if I shall find such a man again." She sighed. "But I must try because I miss physical intimacy terribly."

So, was she propositioning him for sex? Or just making a general observation? It seems threatening to Hardy – the thought that he might be required to 'perform' and then be judged against the dead husband. The woman was just too direct for him. Maybe it was a German trait? He supposed it was better than beating about the bush.

It put him off. This woman was too direct for him. Probably a German trait he told himself, and indeed thinking about it, why beat around the bush?

They parted without making plans to meet again and Hardy was both relieved and disappointed. She had been intimidating, but had he missed a chance to really live?

Christmas came and went. The rules around going to church with worries over Covid 19 were vague and open to interpretation. However, because the mainstream media had done such a good job of alarming both Joyce and Hardy, they decided against attending any service.

What was laughingly called entertainment on the BBC came and went without much notice. Christmas Day and Boxing Day were just days with titles. Joyce had never been so aware of loneliness, a feeling that was enhanced by the media. How many times had she heard that 'everyone' was partying tonight? How many times must she hear that families were all together and having a jolly time?

New Year came and went, no different to any other day apart from getting woken up on New Year's Eve by fireworks. The sirens from the ships in the dockyard over in Portsmouth sounded off at midnight, assuming that everyone was celebrating the crap that had just gone, or perhaps even the crap that was yet to come. Whatever, the noise wakened all, wanting to celebrate or not, you had no option. And then, to sleep again, but no, there would be some loud-mouthed drunk or group making their way back home, drunk on the rent money no doubt, Joyce thought.

CHAPTER TEN

A Cross-Examination

Hardy continued his efforts with online dating. He had not been put off by his previous meeting, realising that most of the problem had been him. He needed to be more free with a woman, not so restrained. Like he had been in the old days. He needed to update his photo, he thought. Perhaps show some of his new improved body after using the rowing machine. Or was the improvement only in his imagination?

"Ah," he thought, "the rowing machine." He had not used it in days, since the novelty had worn off, and it was more in the way than anything else. It was not doing anything other than making him red in the face and out of breath: there was no prospect of it turning him into a first-class athlete. He decided to sell the damned thing. Online would be best, not that he had ever done it before and he certainly wasn't going to ask Joyce's advice. He confidently typed in 'he bay.com' and somehow got Richard Branson selling financial packages. He tried again, 'www.he-bay.co' and got a Japanese site.

So he had to ask Joyce after all.

"It's eBay, you dozy sod." She seemed to sneer at him. "Why do you want to know?"

"I'm going to sell the rowing machine."

"That didn't last long, did it?"

He ignored her as usual, especially due to the fact that she was correct, yet again.

Hardy sat there thinking before ringing his latest contact. Had he really ever been free with women, he wondered? He had been brought up in a time when you behaved with respect, but today things seemed different, with little respect shown to women by younger people. He needed to be more forceful, to demonstrate that he was a real man and not one to be pushed around the way Joyce had treated him.

He had been chatting online to a woman called Penelope. She was 64, divorced and lived in the New Forest close to Southampton.

He had her landline number and had arranged to ring around six in the evening. It was dark, cold and miserable. Joyce was watching something on television, so she wouldn't hear his conversation. He nervously dialled. Even the ring tone seemed to add to the tension.

"Hello." It was a very seductive voice, Hardy thought, sounding a lot younger than her sixty-four years.

"Oh, hello Penelope, it's Hardy here."

"Hello. No, I'm Mabel, I'm her daughter – just a minute and I'll get her for you. You're her online friend, aren't you?"

"I think you could say that. Thanks."

Hardy waited a minute. He could feel his heart thumping, but it appeared the 'appointment' did not hold the same significance to her as it did to him.

"Hello, Hardy. It's Penelope." The voice sounded similar to her daughter's. "How are you?" She sounded friendly and quite relaxed.

"Fine, thanks, and you?"

"Healthwise pretty good, but Mabel's returned home after a break-up in her marriage. While it's nice to have her here, I find I am not used to sharing things nowadays."

Ah, thought Hardy, she's not looking for anything long-term.

"Have you lived on your own for long?"

"Quite some time – my husband was killed on active service in Afghanistan."

That took Hardy by surprise. This woman seemed very open, and quite happy to disclose no end of information in seconds. But she continued before Hardy had chance to reply.

"I'm sorry, I am gabbing on, aren't I? Probably telling you too much too soon. I do this when I am nervous and as you're only the second man I've spoken to as a result of the dating website, I'll level with you and tell you that I am extremely nervous."

"Oh, thank God for that," replied Hardy, somewhat relieved that this was not the one-sided exercise that he thought it might be. "My only dating experiences have been a disaster, so I'm also nervous."

"Thanks for that, at least we have both levelled with each other. I'd never thought of doing this until my daughter moved in just after Christmas. She showed me a few sites that she uses, and that's how I got here today."

"So she uses dating sites already, does she?"

"Oh, don't go there! I won't pretend to understand her at all, but as far as I can ascertain she joined a site for 'affairs'. Can you believe that?"

"I've never heard of that," said Hardy somewhat bemused, but continued in a reassuring tone, "but the young are so different to us. They are happy just to go for casual hook-ups these days."

"I'm glad you said that. It's not something that would appeal to me. I'd like to get to know someone and share conversation and perhaps trips out or something."

Hardy was assessing what sort of woman he was talking to. She struck him as a very conventional woman who was seeking her way in a world that was quite alien to her, in fact a bit like he was doing. He found himself relaxing: this did not require the 'man' thing that he had convinced himself of earlier. Here was a woman he could just talk to and take things at a slower pace. The other factor was that she was not 'left over' from a broken marriage ... but then he was, which was her next question.

"So what are your circumstances? Are you divorced?"

"The position is that we are living apart. We mutually agreed that the marriage had become a habit rather than a marital relationship - you know the sort of thing. We have no children, and I think that probably holds you together a bit more when you do have kids." Hardy had gone into his laboured Suffolk drawl.

"Are you telling me you just got bored with each other?"

"Pretty much, I suppose. But it goes deeper than that. My wife desperately wanted children, and the issue became a running sore in the relationship."

"I've been lucky in that respect, in as much as I have my daughter and I also have a son who is in the Army."

"Is he treading in the footsteps of your husband?"

"Yes, and I'm very proud of him."

"You must be. Do you see much of him?"

"Oh gosh yes, he's home every weekend at the moment. There are not many places where the army is currently deployed," she replied, obviously pleased with the arrangement. "But that's sad about you and your wife and the absence of children. I think you miss out on so much -

not least the number of friends you make taking them to school, the things you learn, the wonder of watching them grow to responsible adults ..."

"Yes, yes, I understand all that," Hardy interrupted, having heard this speech numerous times. And to what effect? They had no children and that was that.

Penelope realised what she was doing, and apologised. Then Hardy heard a click, which slightly annoyed him. It became obvious that Mabel must have been listening into the conversation.

"I need to go," Penelope announced suddenly, almost like the allotted time had been used. But she added: "Will you ring again tomorrow, please?"

Hardy replaced the receiver, relieved that he had navigated this phone call without a car crash. He sat back in his seat, the only sound that of a dull TV playing downstairs in the witch's cauldron. He applied a sense of realism to what had just happened.

Mabel was obviously 'vetting' him, listening into the conversation, spotting the red flags that her 'naive' mother would not have picked up. Had he waved any red flags? He didn't know. Hardy imagined that Mabel and her mother were now discussing and analysing the past five minutes.

"Well mum," he imagined Mabel kicking off, "he has no baggage to speak of, I mean no family at all by the sounds of it, which if you were looking for long-term relationship is a plus. But I'm not sure about the wife, is she 'ex' or is she still current?"

"Oh how terribly liberal of you, darling," Penelope might reply.

"The other thing was that he sounded half asleep. I mean it took him twice as long to say something as anyone else would, almost like he was 'on' something."

"Yes, I noticed that – maybe he's had a stroke or something."

"So, several topics to clear up tomorrow, which you failed to investigate today – his health, his wealth, his physical abilities."

"For God's sake Mabel, all I want is some company of my own age. He told me he still has a business of his own, so he can't be that badly off, and as to his health and what did you call it? Physical abilities? I am hardly going to get an accurate description over the phone, am I?"

Mabel ignored her mother's protestations.

"And then you. You didn't come over as particularly sassy."

"Sassy?"

"Sexy then."

"I didn't intend to on a first conversation, young lady. Thank you for your advice, however, I shall do things my own way."

"Grab life, mum."

That's what Hardy imagined. He, of course, had no one to go over anything with. He presumed if the worst came to the worst he could discuss it with Olly, but Olly was not very good at this sort of thing. In any case, such a conversation would mean full disclosure of the issues with Joyce, and he was not so keen on that, fearing he might be branded some sort of 'inadequate'. Penelope seemed a very nice lady, balanced, and without relationship issues. For the moment, he would pursue this lady, hunt her like a caveman and expose the hidden passions that surely lay within.

He also wrestled with his own position in life. He needed to have more interests, to get out more, to mix with bigger groups, to be sociable. Sitting at home was stifling, bad for his mental health he thought. He mused on the phrase 'mental health'. When he was young, you were either sane or bonkers, and parents, teachers and friends would just tell you to 'pull yourself together' and get on with it.

The call had definitely given him a kick-start. He needed to say to Penelope, or any potential date, that he was doing things *now*, at this moment. He must not rely on the past; he needed to say, for example, that he was representing Gosport at bowls, or writing a book, or indeed had published a book.

What if he got a dog? He had heard that dogs are the easiest way of talking to people, especially if it was the sort of dog that could be called 'cute'.

The morning saw a further call by the police: they seemed less friendly this time.

Hardy was beside himself – he was so enjoying this from his position at the top of the stairs.

"If you remember, Joyce, you told us about witnessing of the transfer of a box from the alleged ex-wife of your date to his car," said the policeman.

"Yes, that's what I told you."

"Did any of the contents of that box find its way into your vehicle?"

"I didn't have a car, I went by train."

The two officers looked at each other, almost quizzically.

"You see the thing is, the man you called Charles is alleging that you knew exactly what was in the box and that you had arranged to meet him in order to pick up a consignment and transport it to Gosport."

"Good God, that's ridiculous, of course I didn't." She was outraged.

"Well, the problem we have also is that you are already

on a charge of causing an affray on the Gosport Ferry. You are not the nice little old lady that you may appear to be, are you?"

"We were all let off with a police caution on that occasion and it was a legitimate protest, I might have you know," she said, indignantly. "Are we to be branded like common criminals now, just for making a protest?"

"Of course not, but of course when we put your name into the police computer, this caution comes up. So, as you are someone on our books, it would be remiss of us not to make further enquiries."

Hardy had been enjoying the proceedings until now: he too had been let off with a caution, but had not appreciated that this left him with a police record. What followed was even worse.

"We need to take a written statement from you which we can do here, or at the Police Station if you prefer."

Joyce actually preferred the Police Station, where Hardy could not earwig at the top of the stairs, but there was something threatening about surrendering herself to a Police Station.

"No, I am happy to do it here – you wish to do it now?" she asked.

"Thank you."

She told them of the date, the fact that she had found Charles online and he had seemed very pleasant. That had been their first meeting, which she had left prematurely.

Hardy was beside himself with laughter, yet felt guilty because it wasn't really funny at all. It was a warning for all of us, he thought, meeting people when you've only known them online. You never really know what you are getting yourself into.

"Amazing isn't it?" said Joyce to the two officers. "For

seventy-two years, I have not so much as even spoken to a policeman, and now I am involved with you twice in nearly as many months."

"I will put your mind at rest, Joyce. While we keep a record of cautions, it's not an actual criminal record. I mean you wouldn't have to declare it if you went to the US, for example."

"Oh, thank goodness for that, I was so worried my trip down Route 66 would be affected," Joyce replied with an edge of sarcasm.

Upstairs, Hardy was equally relieved. He, like Joyce, had not understood the legality of a police caution. The ferry company had called the police after Hardy, Joyce and their accomplices had staged their protest on the ferry, putting up a banner along the railings on the upper deck. They all had been required to attend the police station the day after the event. The police had been more amused than anything else, telling them that the ferry had no wish to pursue any charges, but that the group of pensioners would receive a caution to 'keep the peace'.

However, some three weeks later, the Gosport Harbour Ferry Company had written to all the members of the group, saying that they had abused the terms of passage, and as such the company had decided to withdraw the 'right of passage' during future journeys, for a period of a year.

Joyce was infuriated but Hardy had taken a more pragmatic view, pointing out that hundreds used the ferry every day and their little band of protestors were unlikely to be recognised by the crew.

Joyce found the County Court in Winchester to be an imposing – almost threatening – building, more so perhaps because she was nervous. She was briefed by the Barrister for the 'Crown' who told her that she would only spend five minutes at the most in court, but that there would be a lot of waiting around: justice in UK courts grinds at the pace of a snail. Joyce had been taken aback that the Barrister was dressed in his robes and wig. Did they really still dress like that? The robes had a peculiar smell that she thought was mothballs.

She sat in the court waiting room. In the seat opposite was a man who caught her eye and smiled. He had brown hair greying at the temples and was wearing a suit – he obviously had respect for where he was.

"Which court are you in?" he asked Joyce. His voice was rich and dark. They had all been warned that they were not to discuss the evidence or any details of a case, which made it even harder for Joyce because she was just aching to talk these matters over. But there seemed no harm in telling him the court number.

"I'm in court three, and you?" she said.

"One. I've been told I could be here for some while."

His voice was rather sexy, she thought.

"It's all this hanging around I don't like. I mean, don't these courts realise the disruption they cause to people's lives?"

"It's even worse when you are on jury service," he said. "Very interesting, of course, if you get a case, but the waiting around is deplorable."

"You've been called for jury service in the past?"

"Yes, last year – it amazed me. It was in Portsmouth Crown Court. They have over a hundred people there at a time, so total confusion reigned."

"Over one hundred?" Joyce asked.

"Well, they have to have a choice of jurors for each court – 20 is the figure I think – and there are six courts operating at any one time, so that number soon adds up."

"Gosh, I had never thought of it like that. What sort of case did you get?"

"It was really boring, an assault on a young lad, which a few years ago would have been cleared up by a copper giving them both a clip round the ear and being told to get on with it. Now they get a criminal record that attaches to them for years, stops them getting a job and all sorts of things."

Joyce could relate to that. She had done research into just how far into the criminal justice system she had sailed: one step out of place now and she would officially have a record. As it was, her name just came up on the police computer - totally different to having a record, she had been assured. It didn't feel like that.

Joyce and David exchanged names, he got her a coffee, and she shared a bun with him she had brought from home. They spent an hour in enforced company, before she blurted out the question which she instantly regretted.

"So, are you married?"

But he was quite willing to share such information with her.

"No not now. I had been married for thirty-something years but she developed a form of early-onset dementia. She died a year ago after being in a home for about six months. It was not a pleasant experience."

Joyce was almost overcome with sympathy. Her experience was nothing like that.

"I am so sorry, I didn't mean to intrude."

"It's OK. I need to be able to talk about it, so I am told."

"Yes, I guess so, but not in the circumstances that we both find ourselves in today."

"What about you?" David asked.

Joyce did not hesitate: "I'm on my own as well. My husband and I have split up after years of marriage."

"That's sad," he said.

"Oh I don't know, we drove each other mad – it was a blessed relief in the end and I think we are both happier now."

"Do you still see him?"

"Occasionally." Joyce wondered if that was a lie, or just not explaining the truth.

"There must be lots to sort out when you have been married for so long."

Joyce wasn't really sure how to answer that, as she had not actually gone through any of the machinations of real separation or divorce. She just nodded.

"We should talk more," he said.

It was as if this was choreographed. The Usher called him, he quickly scribbled his phone number on a paper serviette, and asked her to ring him later.

She did. The day in court had been awful. When she had been called, she did not recognise the man in the dock. Charles had cut his hair, was wearing a suit, and was bespectacled. No doubt a ruse for the court, she thought. But why is he in the dock, she wondered? The police had led her to believe it was Debs they were after. She had no idea what was going on.

The prosecution took her through her evidence, just as had been arranged, but what Joyce had not bargained on was being cross-examined by the defence.

"Would you say that you have good eyesight?"

"Fairly good. I do wear glasses though, as you can see."

"So not that good," he said with a smirk. That wound Joyce up.

"You are an optician then?" she came back at him. The jury chuckled but the Judge asked Joyce to just answer the questions.

"The point I am making," said the defence lawyer, "is that it must have been difficult for you to see exactly what was going on, through a dirty window and at dusk."

"I am not in the habit of lying. I saw what I saw and I have told the court the absolute truth. I have not elaborated anything, or left out anything." Joyce was cross. Her integrity was being challenged and she didn't like that.

"Madam, I am trying to get to the truth. It is necessary to find out whether you may have been mistaken or even believed you saw something that you actually didn't."

Joyce ignored that remark: it wasn't a question so it required no response.

"Well did you?" he enquired eventually.

"How on earth can I answer a question like that? If I didn't believe I saw something that I did see but didn't notice, I wouldn't have seen it, would I?"

It took a while for the court to understand her response, and when they did there were a few smiles from the jury, but not from old misery guts with his wig; he was still unimpressed with Joyce. His expression remained ice-cold, but then, Joyce reasoned with herself, this was just another day at the office for him and the others.

"You live in Gosport, correct?" the defence lawyer continued.

"Yes, I do."

"Can you explain to the court why you were sitting in an empty cafe attached to a theatre in Basingstoke at five in the evening, meeting with this couple?"

Joyce had given no thought to the possibility that a question like this might be asked. Could she get away with a 'cover-all' answer?

"I had personal reasons."

Not enough.

"Can you explain those personal reasons?"

"I'd rather not."

The judge then intervened. He addressed her and explained that because the case relied on statements from the accused that implicated her, it was necessary to allow the jury to understand why she was there in the first place. Joyce realised that she had little choice.

"Well, my husband and I have recently separated, and in an effort to find company and perhaps another partner, I joined an online dating site. It was on that site that I met Charles, and we arranged a date over the telephone."

The prosecution lawyer now stood.

"Your Honour, I think you will find that the police have already collaborated that, in so much as the online activity and phone records have been checked."

There followed an exchange in which it appeared that the court accepted that Joyce had been in the wrong place at the wrong time and that no blame could be attributed to her. Joyce had expected sniggers from the jury, but none came.

The inane questions continued.

"So, this was the first time you had met the defendant in person?"

"Yes."

"Can you please explain to the court the gist of your conversation?"

Joyce relayed what little she could remember, and then explained that Charles's ex-wife arrived.

"I knew we were due to watch her perform that evening, but when she arrived in the car park, Charles became almost ecstatic with excitement. I did at that point wonder what on earth was going on. I mean, who brings an ex-wife on a date with another potential partner?"

At this, the jury did laugh, and even the judge smiled.

"When she arrived in the cafe, I believe you left."

"Not quite, she told me about Charles, and along with his peculiar behaviour earlier on, I decided it was better for me to leave."

The court also heard that the conversation with the ex-wife was about Charles' autism and that he had an inability to understand the emotions of other people.

Joyce did not hang around for the verdict: she was told by the Usher that she would not be needed again, and so she shot out of the place like a bullet leaving the barrel of a gun.

The weather was now very wintery, cold and rainy. She had taken the train to Winchester; it was tedious, stopping at every conceivable station known to man. However, coming back, she made the mistake of nodding off, and when she woke up she was looking at Fratton station, way past her destination of Fareham. She decided to stay on the train right through to Portsmouth Harbour, then get the ferry back to Gosport. True to form, she missed a ferry by about two minutes. As she waited on the old and grubby Portsmouth pontoon, she thought back to that hot sunny day when she and her group of friends and revolutionaries had drunk coffee on the station platform, waiting for their return trip on the ferry. It had been there that she had first learnt of Bert's illness.

She took out her phone, which was wrapped in the serviette on which David had written his number. She could ring him. Instead, she texted him, asking if he was free to speak and he replied in double-quick time, saying that he would call her.

Her phone rang to the tune of Land of Hope and Glory. She did find it a bit embarrassing as a woman in the queue turned and stared at her, so she tried to answer it quickly.

Their conversation was a lot more relaxed than the dating-site phone calls. Joyce felt like she already knew David – after all, they had already chatted for just over an hour.

He wanted to take her out to dinner and was happy to drive to Gosport to do so. Perhaps their conversation in the court's waiting room had been an old-fashioned chat-up?

CHAPTER ELEVEN
Say Hello to Uncle Joe

Hardy was more than happy with his date with Penelope, arranged soon after their first phone call. She was nice and she was, as far as he could tell, pretty normal in her approach to life. She obviously was comfortable financially, and seemed to have a normal relationship with her daughter. In fact, it was all pretty normal. Hardy asked himself whether 'normal' equated to 'boring'. Perhaps he should use his time pursuing someone a bit younger and more different?

His dating site held lots of women, many of them younger than forty-five and many of them asking for older men. He found that odd. What would younger women see in older men? Cash, security and perhaps manners, he quickly realised. But he could be taking advantage of the opportunity – Penelope would never know and anyway, it would only be for a bit of fun.

In her profile picture, the woman he had picked out had black hair and looked slim although the photograph was just head and shoulders. Why had Hardy noticed her in particular? She had temptingly naked shoulders in the picture, which led him to the possibility that she was not wearing anything else. She said she was forty-one, and she might well have been at the time of the photograph, thought Hardy.

'I'm getting too cynical,' he said to himself. 'The only way of finding things out for sure is to meet these women. I'm an experienced enough guy not to be taken advantage of.'

Her name was Lucy and she lived in Portsmouth

"Very handy, living just over the Harbour," said Hardy out loud.

He thought he would contact her and just check things out. It felt like a new departure: he'd not initiated a chat on a dating site with anyone so young.

When they were exchanging texts, Hardy realised that he was old enough to be her father and suddenly had doubts about the situation. But he decided to call her and at least go over to see her. He always felt the need to shout into mobile phones, as if using the old military ones on a battlefield. Lucy asked very little, just whether it was OK for Hardy to come to her house, which Hardy found surprising because all the advice – especially for women – was usually to meet in a public place. She had a strong Portsmouth accent that was quite unlike the middle-class public-school clarity of Penelope's accent.

Hardy agreed that he would go to see her the following day, at around six-thirty. When he boarded the ferry, the crew member greeted him.

"Hope you're not hijacking us tonight, eh?"

"No, I don't think that's on the cards."

"Look mate, you know you're not meant to be on here – the company has refused permission for you to board."

Hardy had banked on not being recognised, but obviously he was more famous, or infamous than he realised. He doubted whether they could legally enforce the ban, but if he was not allowed on board now, he was going to have to drive round – that meant getting to Lucy's late.

The crew member relented.

"Go on mate, I haven't recognised you. OK?"

"Thanks." Hardy waddled on.

Lucy's place was upstairs, a maisonette in a block of about thirty-two other dwellings not far from the ferry, up Queen's Street. He needed to negotiate a semi-covered walkway that led to Lucy's front door. In doing so, he passed four other maisonettes. A dog barked as he passed the first one, while attacking the letter box.

"Shut up! Shut up!" he heard from inside.

"Can't you shut that bleedin' dog up?"

Hardy passed quickly. There were smells, smells of cooking, hot oil and sausages. There were other smells not quite as pleasant. There were kids screaming in an upstairs bedroom, obviously a punch-up over some inconsequential dispute. But there it was, the front door. Directly to his right, the number thirty-six stared at him. That in itself was not alarming – what was alarming was that the noise from the kids was emanating directly above where he was standing. Perhaps it was a trick of sound – perhaps it wasn't even in this block. It was sound that reverberated amongst the densely constructed flats and maisonettes.

There was no bell. He tried the letter box, which even with force could only produce a muffled attention-seeking flapping noise. He reverted to banging on the glass of the door. This time the door half opened, and a face appeared in the gap. He thought she was reluctant to open up, but the real reason became abundantly clear within seconds as an out-of-control rabid dog attempted a series of escapes from the property, with what he assumed was Lucy trying to restrain it. Eventually she said:

"Just a minute, I'll put him in the kitchen."

With that, the door closed again, leaving Hardy alone in

the passageway again. It was not long before the door opened fully, and standing in front of him was the woman he assumed was Lucy. There was a resemblance to her online photo, but she had been through the wars since the photo had been taken. She had black hair, but her roots indicated that she coloured it. She was wearing jeans and a huge sloppy jumper; it was orange, but had marks on it that indicated it had been a long time since it had seen a wash. And then the smell hit. A mixture of dog and cigarette. He detected none of the fragrance of Penelope.

"Hi, Hardy. Come in." She beckoned.

Hardy was no longer sure about this, but to do an about-turn now would appear very rude indeed, and that was not in his nature. He crossed the threshold into a world of turmoil quite different to anything he had ever encountered. There was a scooter on the floor, there were coats hanging on the banister and some had fallen off onto the floor. The dog was now scraping at what Hardy assumed was the kitchen door.

A child's voice shouted down the stairs.

"Who's that?" It sounded like a girl's voice.

"None of your business, get ready for bed and then you can play on your iPad."

That had no effect. A girl of about ten came hurtling down the stairs. She made an enormous amount of noise in doing so as there was no stair carpet.

"Get back up! Get back up now!" Lucy shouted.

"I only wanted to see who it was, who is he?" She stared at Hardy.

"I told you, none of your business."

"Is he going to be another uncle?"

"Get up!" Lucy was furious. She turned to Hardy: "Pain in the arse, those two," she said.

Hardy did not really know how to respond to that, but continued to tread over stuff to the door at the end of the corridor that was obviously led to the lounge. Again, it smelt of cigarettes and dog. He was offered the settee, which had seen better days. The arm was black and had gone what he would call 'crusty', though the original colour had obviously been red. As he sat, he needed to remove a model car. There was a chair next to the settee, pointing towards a huge television that at the moment was displaying a picture without sound. It was the news: he reasoned, quite without evidence, that it would not be of interest to her. Lucy sat in the chair next to him.

"Can I get you a drink?" she asked.

"That would be nice." Hardy could do with a drink.

"What's your poison? I got wine or vodka."

"I'll have a glass of wine please."

"I should have brought you something, I am very sorry, that was very remiss of me, I guess I am not used to this."

"No worries," she replied, getting up to go to a sideboard that was covered with toys and other random objects.

She opened a bottle of red, got out a wine glass and then proceeded to fill it to the brim.

He said nothing, but he always felt the glass needed to be big enough so you could swill the wine to get some air into it. She reached into the sideboard again, this time bringing out about a bottle of vodka three-quarters full. She poured herself a triple.

"Thank you," Hardy said as he took the wine. "As I said, I am a bit new to this and a bit nervous – are you?"

"No, I'm not new to it – been out with about six blokes I suppose, but I'm always nervous. See," and she pointed to the vodka.

"Yes."

"I nearly always meet men here. With the dog and kids here, I figure that I'm as safe as anywhere. It's so difficult to get a baby sitter and it's so bleeding expensive as well."

"Is it? I've never had children."

"Really? That's unusual – to get a bloke without baggage."

"Don't let me mislead you, I do have baggage – as you call it – in the shape of an ex-wife."

"Yeah of course, any geezer of your age that ain't been married is a bit suspect."

"You been married?" Hardy queried.

"No, had a common-law guy, but he's inside now."

"Inside?"

"Wandsworth."

Hardy was taken aback by that.

"What did he do to warrant that?"

"What?"

"What did he do to warrant … get sentenced to prison?" Hardy figured she had a problem with the word 'warrant'.

"He got done for GBH - some guy tried it on with me one night and he got jealous. But it ain't the first time; he runs on a short fuse."

"So how long did he get, I mean when does he get out?"

"He's still got a year to do, and don't worry, he ain't coming anywhere near us again. It's all over, not worth the aggro."

Hardy was perturbed as to what he was getting into here. He took a gulp of his wine.

"What about you then," she said. "You still see the missus?"

"Yes, I still see her, but she is with another man now."

"So you thought you would try a younger bit … yeah?"

"Went through my mind, I cannot lie." By now, and after a few gulps of wine, Hardy thought he had nothing to lose. If she became offended, so what? He would get up and go. But she did not seem offended.

"Where do I fit into that, then?"

"Well, you're younger aren't you?" he said. "You said you were forty-one." She had finished her first vodka already. "Bloody hell, you can put it away, can't you?"

"Can I? You don't have a clue, do you? You don't have a soddin' clue."

"A soddin' clue about what?" said Hardy, as he took the last gulp of wine, hoping for a refill. She obliged, recharging both their glasses.

"A soddin' clue as to how I live, what it's like. Look, do you really think a girl of my age is attracted to you sexually, eh? Nah, I'm looking for security in return for the odd shag."

There was a knock at the door, more successful than Hardy's first attempt because it set the dog going straight away.

"Bloody hell," was Lucy's response followed by "Fey! Fey! See who that is."

"What?" was the response from the girl, shouting from the top of the stairs.

"See who it is at the door, will you? I'm busy."

"Why can't Charlie?"

"Cause he can't reach the bloody door handle yet. Just do it."

Fey, moaning, stamped her way down the stairs to open the front door. Hardy heard voices, and then the sound of feet running towards the lounge door.

Fey was no more than ten. She was wearing grubby tracksuit pyjamas and had lovely black hair like her mother.

"It's Uncle Joe. He asked if he could see you a min."

Lucy ignored Hardy as if he wasn't there.

"Tell him no, tell him he can't keep coming round like this."

Hardy thought this to be totally inappropriate. The child should not have to convey such a message to a man left at the door.

"He's got flowers for you," Fey added in an attempt to get her mother to deal with it.

"Oh for Christ's sake." Lucy seemed exasperated, and eventually got up. She offered no 'excuse me' to Hardy; she just left the room.

The mumbled voices went on for what seemed ages but it was probably only two minutes before she returned to the lounge. She was carrying what looked to Hardy like a very expensive bunch of flowers.

"Look, aren't they gorgeous?"

"Lovely. I guess he is another one of your suitors."

"What?"

"Have you seen him before?"

"Oh yeah, several times, but he's out of order when he comes round here uninvited. I told him it's not on, but Fey said he could come in and play."

Hardy thought this sounded bizarre and even a bit dodgy.

"In their bedroom? Is that sensible?"

"Well it keeps them both quiet – they really get on with him and he's harmless."

"That may be the case, but you can't be too careful."

"What d'you mean 'can't be too careful'? What sort of mother do you think I am? He's OK and at least he looks after us … to a degree. He bought us that telly last month. I know he's a pain keep coming round, but I can't send him

136

back without him seeing the kids at least. He knows you're here."

"Right, so he's upstairs and I'm down here - this isn't an ideal situation is it?" Hardy, as if a bolt of lightning had hit him, realised what he had just said: upstairs/downstairs. How ironic!

"Yeah," said Lucy, "but I suspect he'll stay on, if you know what I mean."

Hardy came to his senses. Basically, the woman was not much different to a prostitute. Was he expected to pay for it tonight? No way. Kids in the house, rabid dog, man upstairs, boyfriend in prison, and now he had drunk some of her cheap wine.

"I need to go, I think," he said.

"Do you?" Lucy seemed genuinely surprised. "Don't you like meeee?" she added, now beginning to slur her words.

"Yes I do like you," he lied, but not wishing to upset her. "I just don't feel comfortable with him upstairs."

"Do you want me to tell him to take a walk for a while then?" She seemed almost desperate to keep Hardy from leaving.

"No, of course not. That's rude."

"Naaa, he's bloody rude coming round like this. He knows I sometimes have … guests."

That remark confirmed it with Hardy. He was now sure he was going to be asked to leave her a 'gift' of cash. He headed for the door of the lounge, almost panicking. He opened it and what greeted him was unnerving. There stood the man who was meant to be upstairs, obviously listening at the door. But what shocked Hardy was that this man was the spitting image of Bert. Round, short – even his clothes resembled those that Bert would have worn.

"Christ!" was Hardy's involuntary expletive.

"Sorry, I was going to see if either of you wanted a drink," replied 'Uncle Joe'. It was clearly a lie.

"You remind me of an old friend, who sadly is no longer with us," Hardy explained. He pushed past Joe in the crowded corridor: he just wanted out. He got to the front door.

"Thanks for your hospitality," he said, rather lamely, to Lucy.

Lucy was standing in the doorway of the lounge, looking bewildered and a little worse for wear.

"Go on then, fuck off."

She had become angry in seconds. Hardy quickly shut the front door on the scene. He reasoned the quicker he was gone, the better. Even the stairs seemed threatening. He imagined she was on the phone to thugs downstairs that would beat him up for her. But thankfully, he escaped unharmed.

The Gosport Ferry suddenly seemed like a safe haven. As he approached, he could see it just leaving the Gosport side. He wanted to get back over the water as quickly as possible. Gosport could be seen, lights just coming on. The old submarine escape tower loomed over the HMS Dolphin site and the two blocks of tall flats seemed permanent and comforting. He picked up his pace slightly and was actually out of breath by the time he arrived on the pontoon.

He waited whilst the ferry berthed. There was only about six other people waiting. Hardy was last to board.

"You're banned, mate," said the crew member, not the one he had seen on the journey over.

"What d'you mean? I was allowed over."

"Don't care, mate, my instructions are not to let you on – you cause trouble, I'm told."

"Well I never caused any trouble coming over from Gosport."

"Sorry but you shouldn't have been let on over there. What time did you come over?"

Hardy was not saying; he had no intention of getting anyone into trouble. Instead he just said: "OK, if that's your attitude, I'll just have to go round on the bus then."

And with that he laboured back up the pontoon. The tide was right out and the slope made his walk even slower. It did go through his mind that the man from the ferry might even feel a bit sorry for him and call him back but he didn't.

"Bastard," he muttered under his breath.

Luckily there was a bus to Fareham in its bay and some two hours later, he arrived back home in Gosport. He felt knackered. The last person he wanted to see as he staggered back through the door was Joyce.

"You've had a phone call," she announced with a slight grin on her face.

"Who?"

"Someone from the Salvation Army, who said they would ring back another time."

"From the Salvation Army?" Hardy queried.

"That's what they said. Trying to save your soul, I expect."

CHAPTER TWELVE
A Ghastly Coincidence

Joyce's relationship with David was going well; he was a really nice man although she remained very aware that he was nine years younger than her. He made her feel good, and that was the main thing. She was due to meet him that afternoon. She thought how 'senior' that was, inasmuch as most of their dates had been at lunchtime. She had asked him about work, but he said he had no need to work any longer: he had enough savings behind him and a pension that he had drawn early.

She had noticed that Hardy was also missing from the house most lunchtimes, so perhaps he was meeting someone too …. or perhaps just going out on his own to have lunch.

He was still using the car. Joyce had not driven much of late, so access to the car didn't bother her in itself, but the principle did. Hardy was – in her mind – assuming ownership, and that was not on.

She was still wrestling with all the other problems of their living arrangements. She was tempted to come clean with David and be honest about the arrangement with Hardy. She had never lied about it to David, but hadn't told him the whole truth either. If she did explain it, would he perceive it as not being a true separation? But then she argued that if David was developing feelings for her, he would accept the situation and would accept everything she told him. The other question she needed to sort out in her head was the important one of whether she was developing feelings for David beyond just liking him. She just didn't know. She sprayed Chanel across her shoulders: the perfume always made her s feel a bit more feminine. Perhaps David was producing some reaction within her that she was unaware of? Certainly, she was feeling young, or youngish, again. Something was stirring.

Hardy was thumping around upstairs. He must be getting heavier, Joyce thought, because the floorboards were creaking more than normal. It was just as the creaking was beginning to really annoy her again that she heard a massive thud, and a shout from Hardy offering a crude Anglo-Saxon expletive. Her first reaction was to shout up the stairs: this was a normal human caring for another she thought, she was big enough to do that.

"Are you OK?" Joyce shouted.

"No, I'm bloody not!"

Well at least he's conscious thought Joyce. Can't be that serious.

"What have you done?"

There was a pause, "I've kicked a chair in bare feet and it bloody well hurts."

"Oh, is that all?" Was she disappointed, she asked herself? Dreadful thoughts went through her mind that perhaps a heart attack might end all of this for both of them. That was awful, she thought – too much!

Hardy was readying himself to meet Penelope for lunch. He was to meet her locally this time: for their first date, they'd met at a café in the New Forest and he had decided to explain his living arrangements.

He was finding himself more and more attracted to her, to her grace and poise ... and to her obvious financial security. That was important because it meant she would not be one of these women just after his money. She had told him that she was adequately looked after by the Ministry of Defence who gave her a special payment and pension, and along with other small sources of income, she was well provided for. Hardy was always careful when she brought up the subject of her husband; after all, the man had been killed in the service of the country and had been honoured for it, so a certain respect was required. He doubted whether she would have that much respect for him, never having had a service career, never having really done much that counted towards 'masculinity'. He also sometimes felt a bit dim when talking to her. She was very cultured and had a good knowledge of literature. Hardy was not well read, unless it was a Haynes car manual.

Penelope was slightly shorter than Joyce, but she had the same blonde hair which she permed. She was always smartly dressed in what appeared to Hardy to be 'classy' clothes. Unlike Joyce she did not wear spectacles, although Hardy did wonder whether she wore contact lenses. Her build was slight, whereas in Hardy's eyes Joyce had become slightly bulky.

Their conversations had, at first, been laboured and they had tended to keep to general topics like the weather and her journey to the venue. They had once strayed into Brexit, finding common ground, because they had both been on the leave side. She explained how her daughter was an avid 'remainer' and that they had fallen out over it for some while. Penelope thought the reason was generational. Many young people had known nothing else and the freedom to live or work on the Continent anywhere from Finland to Malta was something they all valued. Penelope was also a Parish Councillor. That made sense, thought Hardy. She seemed very popular with her neighbours, and when he had met her in the cafe on their first date, she had been greeted by half the people who walked in.

All in all, he wondered whether he was a bit out of his depth, but he did fancy her, and thought if the conditions were right he might be able to 'have his way' with her. He knew that a number of things had to come together for that to happen: the right place, the right time, the right inclination on both their parts ... and of course for the right assisting medication being available half an hour beforehand. It all sounded like too much trouble.

Hardy had been keen to show her some of Gosport, a town that, despite the fact she had lived in the South of England for most of her life, she had never set foot in. She had driven along the seafront of Lee-on-the-Solent, past the Hovercraft museum and on past what remained of the old pier following Hardy's directions to the restaurant that was right next to the Gosport Marina. An impressive site greeted Penelope: great views of Portsmouth Harbour.

"Hi, Hardy," she said as she got out of the car. She was her usual happy self and Hardy did his best to reciprocate.

"Great to see you again. You found your way here without any problems?"

"Yes. It was really nice driving along the seafront, and the sea is here again. I actually stopped for a couple of minutes. And that airfield, with those little planes in and out every few minutes, seems ever so busy."

Hardy had never really noticed them, so just nodded.

"And I am guessing that the clearance in the trees over

on the island was Osborne House?"

"Yes … if you were looking in the right place, that is. There's a pub back along the road beyond Lee-on-the-Solent called the Osborne View. We'll have to go there sometime."

They walked into the The Deck. Hardy was wearing his old brown jacket and cord trousers, and suddenly felt a little underdressed.

"I never know what to wear," he said. He was aware that she seemed to have clothes for any occasion, and it jarred a little that his wardrobe was drab.

"You're fine," she reassured him. But then Hardy was aware that she would say that anyway – that was the class of the woman.

The Deck was a standard-fayre establishment with a predictable menu of fish and chips and salads, and the odd burger thrown into the mix. Somewhere, Hardy thought, that things could not really go wrong.

All was going fine until he spotted another couple, at first admiring the view and then entering the restaurant: Joyce, accompanied by a man.

The man was tall and had a 'service' type haircut, short back and sides. He was still wearing sunglasses, so Hardy couldn't see his face, but he was clean-shaven with long greying sideburns that didn't really go with his hairstyle. He was wearing a shirt and tie, but no jacket.

"Bloody 'ell, what's she doing here?" He meant to just think it, but said it out loud.

"Sorry?" Penelope gave Hardy chance to gather himself. It was obvious he had become suddenly flustered.

"Sorry. Oh bloody hell, it's just that I've noticed who's just come in."

"Is there a problem?"

"It's my wife, well, separated wife and she has some chap with her." Hardy could see the entrance, but Penelope was facing the other way, so without being obvious and turning one hundred and eighty degrees, she had to have the situation described to her.

"Well, you're here with me – nothing wrong with what either of you are doing, is there?"

Hardy hardly heard her. He had gone off into a blind panic of his own. What if they sat at the next table? What was he going to say, how should he introduce Penelope? His brain was going into overdrive.

"For goodness sake, Hardy, calm down." She as obviously irritated.

So far, Joyce had not noticed them. Should he duck to keep his head down? No, of course not; that would be terrible for Penelope, and would look stupid.

"I'm sorry, but them coming in here has just caught me off guard. You know that old line? Of all the joints in all the world, she walks into mine."

"I'm guessing this is the first time you have seen her with someone else."

"Yes."

"And is it hurting you?"

Although used to Joyce's barbed questions, he thought this one was a bit below-the-belt, but the look on her face told him it was genuine, not intended to trick him or to score points. This was new territory for Hardy.

"I really don't know," Hardy responded.

"I think that is probably a very honest answer."

Joyce and David were ushered to seats just two tables away. Joyce spotted Hardy and put her hand involuntarily to her mouth. She too was disturbed, Hardy could see that, but her man was already holding a seat for her that faced away from Hardy and Penelope. That was some consolation. Joyce was now leaning into her 'date' across the table, obviously telling him that her husband was behind her. The man had immediately looked over at Hardy, probably summing up his opposition.

"Look, I don't want to sit here all through lunch with you staring over at them, that's not very enjoyable for me, is it?" Penelope said.

"Of course not, this is something I need to cope with and I am not backing down from it."

Things went back to normal when the waitress asked if they were ready to order. The problem was that Hardy's appetite had completely disappeared. Nevertheless he ordered them a bottle of wine and fish and chips for himself.

"Look, she is probably feeling the same as you are." Penelope pointed out.

"Probably, but then she has a twisted sense of humour."

"And that's what you should have, you should see the funny side of this situation. I mean, to be honest, this is hilarious. I could dine out on this. Not that I intend to of course," she added hastily.

Hardy realised that what she was saying was right. Joyce was ignoring him anyway, and the whole lunch could proceed like that; he could pretend they were not even there. He resolved to pay full attention to Penelope.

The waitress brought the wine but did not pour it; that was left to Hardy. He had ordered a Spanish red, trying to impress and paying what seemed a lot of money for it. He made a play of smelling it; he didn't know why he was smelling it, but he had seen it done many times on television, and it seemed the thing to do. He splashed some into her glass.

"Not too much, Hardy, remember I am driving."

Did that give him an opening? Could he say she could stay at his place overnight? No he couldn't, he didn't have the guts yet, and in any case it would not feel right. It also meant that he could slurp most the bottle if he wanted too, which would help him get through the afternoon. He needed another glass almost immediately, but was aware that he became not terribly good company if he drank too much. He had a tendency to nod off, too. At least the second glass was settling him down, until he spotted – standing at the door waiting to be seated – their joint friends from church, Ken and Sarah.

Why here, why today? This was even worse than Joyce being here, how were they going to explain this situation?

Ken spotted Hardy first.

"Hi, Hardy. Alright?" Hardy had always felt that was a weird greeting. What if he did explain to Ken that this was so far from being alright.

"Hello, Ken. This is a friend of mine, Penelope."

Ken stuck out a hand, introducing Sarah as well.

So far, neither Ken nor Sarah had spotted Joyce. Hardy wondered if Joyce had heard the voices and recognised them, and had decided not to turn round at any cost.

Ken and Sarah decided to sit at the table right opposite Hardy and Penelope so that their conversation could continue.

"Is this OK, or do you guys need some space?" Clearly a loaded question from Ken.

"Of course, please do." What else could Hardy say, as he gulped another half glass of wine?

This seating situation meant that Ken was facing both Sarah and Penelope, and that Sarah was immediately to the back of Joyce. Hardy was in the position of observing the ongoing 'train crash'. It happened when Sarah removed her coat to put over the back of her chair, disturbing the lady behind her, who was leaning across her table towards her companion.

"Oh sorry." Sarah apologised to the woman.

It was then, then, right at that moment, that the train crash happened.

"Joyce! Wow! Hello," said Sarah, appearing a little bemused.

Ken, being a gentleman of sorts, stood to greet the other half of their friendship.

"Hello," said Joyce, twisting uncomfortably round in her seat. She had no option now other than to acknowledge the cast now fully forming.

Penelope seemed more amused now. Her irritated face had gone and something like a smirk replaced it. Joyce did not introduce David, but Ken, being a smooth talker, a talent that had obtained him lots of money in previous years, introduced himself. Ken had stood and walked to the table, giving Joyce a peck on the cheek.

"This is nice," Ken said. "Fancy seeing you all here! Let's ask for a table together, shall we?" Hardy reckoned that Ken knew exactly what he was doing and was about to enjoy an afternoon's entertainment at his and Joyce's cost.

Penelope had to stuff her napkin against her mouth to muffle her fits of laughter.

"Yes, why not have a table together?" she exclaimed, much to Hardy's horror.

Joyce piped up:

"Well we were hoping to have a private conversation."

"Oh to hell with that, let's all just muck in," said David.

Even Joyce wondered what on earth was going on here. Their respective dates were volunteering to dine with two people they had never met. Perhaps that said something about their quality of conversation. But it was too late: Ken was arranging with the waitress for a transfer to a table for six.

"Well, this is fun," said Ken waving a wine glass in the air.

Somehow Ken was seated opposite Joyce and Hardy opposite Sarah, leaving David, who was next to Joyce, opposite Penelope.

Ken continued: "What's the occasion then, or is this just all a coincidence?"

"Oh, totally coincidence." Hardy's speech was already starting to slow down, thanks to the alcohol. Joyce recognised the signs; he was drinking from his wine glass frequently and on an empty stomach, and now Ken had ordered another bottle to be put on the table. Her fears were, of course, that he would show both her and himself up.

Hardy desperately wanted to be next to Penelope, but had found himself next to Joyce and as far away on the same table as it was possible to get from Penelope.

"Are you celebrating anything, Ken?" asked Joyce.

"God no, we come here quite often because we can walk – it's nice to have a wine and meal without having to think about driving."

"That's good that you can walk to a place like this," said Penelope.

"Are you not close to an eatery or pub?" asked Ken.

"No, I live in the New Forest. The nearest pub is about five miles away, so unless my daughter and I cycle to it, I have to drive."

"It must be so nice cycling in the New Forest," said David.

"It is."

The conversation started to flow, but between David and

Penelope. Hardy found himself talking to Sarah about the issues raised by the protest on the ferry. Joyce was stuck with Ken, but it didn't go unnoticed by her that David and Penelope were in deep conversation.

By the time the main courses had been consumed, Hardy was almost out of it and was drifting off to some other world. Sarah had given up on him and turned her attention to Ken.

Joyce, keen to develop the relationship with David, turned to him but found herself an onlooker to a conversation about the New Forest. David obviously knew it well, which he had not mentioned to her previously. He was explaining to Penelope about the importance of the Forest during the Second World War.

"There are so many war graves scattered in the cemeteries from Ringwood, all down the western side of Southampton Water. It really is an eye-opener, and I've been attempting to find back-stories to the people lying in those graves."

"What a fantastic thing to do. I bet that is really interesting," Penelope responded.

Joyce's attempts to add to the conversation were largely falling on stony ground. She really didn't have that much to offer, knowing hardly anything about the New Forest. She could try and change the topic of conversation to something she did know something about, but both David and Penelope were becoming so animated with each other it was going to be difficult. She was beginning to be irritated, but then, out of the blue, she suddenly had something to do.

"Pass me the wine, girl," Hardy begged. The wine had not been touched by the two who were driving, but in the passing, Joyce filled her glass before Hardy got to it.

Neither Ken nor Sarah queried what was going on with

the foursome who had been sitting at different tables when they came in. Sarah had assumed that perhaps the place had been full and they had taken the only two tables.

"Don't be so wet," Ken had whispered to her. "Something really peculiar going on here."

He was on the verge of asking when Hardy announced:

"Well, if you don't mind, Penelope, I was going to show you some of Gosport." He had to lean right across the table to say it, but the statement made it clear that he wanted this little gathering to end. Penelope was no idiot, of course. The last thing she wanted was Hardy in his current state sitting in her car, probably drooling all over her, stinking of booze, or an even worse scenario of throwing up.

"Shall we ask for the bill?" Hardy said to no one in particular, in yet another effort to break up this little party.

Strangely the only one who answered was Joyce in the affirmative. All the others were engaged in conversation.

Hardy sat there, bewildered, when in quite a friendly and not off-hand way, Penelope informed him that as David needed a lift home, she had offered to take him.

"I'll be in touch," she said almost cheerfully. "But we must get off now."

"Oh, right." was about all Hardy could bring himself to say. The humiliation was not lost on him, neither was it lost on Joyce.

"I hope you understand," continued Penelope, "but it still gets dark around five and I hate driving in the dark as you know."

Hardy did know.

David said his farewells to Joyce, thanking her for a lovely time. Turning to Ken and Sarah, he shook hands, also offering his hand to Hardy. Hardy had no axe to grind with this David; he saw no reason than to other than friendly. He reached for David's hand, which was some distance above Hardy's now very laid-back figure. It meant he had to move, and that was a mistake. Hardy lunged for the hand and missed. The momentum of his lunging body took his torso towards the table, and he was unable to avert a collision with a still half-drunk glass of red wine. The tablecloth soaked up some, and so did his white shirt. Ken came to pick Hardy up, and put him back in his chair to 'rest'.

"Oh dear, well, no point in crying over spilt milk, is there?"

"There is when it's red," Joyce said.

The assembled company seemed to find that funny. The usual thing happened. David assembled a quantity of napkins from different unused tables to soak up the wine, but it was left to an embarrassed Joyce to dab paper on Hardy's protruding belly. The whole incident prevented the departure by a good five minutes. The restaurant was almost empty, and was very understanding about the spilt wine. Penelope and David left.

"Bloody cheek!" Hardy suddenly exclaimed, brought back to life by the arrival of the bill.

Ken, Sarah and Joyce both looked at him somewhat bemused.

"What's up?" Ken asked.

"They've both gone off, leaving sweet f.a. towards the bill."

Joyce looked around, expecting to see some banknotes lying on the table, but there were none. She quickly summed up the situation and found herself agreeing with Hardy for once.

"So who are they?" asked Sarah, never one to hold back.

Joyce looked at Hardy, and Hardy looked at Joyce. Both pretty much thought the same: there was no point in holding back. Joyce explained, matter-of factly:

"It will come as no surprise to you that Hardy and I have found difficulties in our relationship, so much so that we now live apart, but in the same house. However, that arrangement allows us to explore other relationships, mainly through online introductions, and to cut a long story short, we were with separate dates in this same pub."

Ken found it hard to keep a straight face, but Sarah found the words:

"That's a bit off isn't it, your two dates buggering off without paying?"

"Hang on Sarah," said Ken, "that's hardly the issue is it? Joyce has just explained that they are going through a hard time, and all you can think about it is the cash."

"True, sorry," she apologised.

Hardy was flustered; this new turn of events, the 'sweeping of the floor' so to speak, was difficult for him to cope with.

"If you want my opinion, and you probably don't, I think you are both mad. Without each other, you will both fall apart." Ken gave his view, welcome or not.

"Well they are still in the same house," Sarah chipped in, almost comforting.

"That may be the way you will work this through," Ken suggested.

Joyce and Hardy sat there, saying nothing, almost like they were being counselled.

"What we going to do about this bill?" Hardy asked Joyce.

Joyce hesitated.

"Well we haven't got a choice, have we? If we ever want to come in here again, we are going to have to pay it."

"Shouldn't we help a little, Ken?" Sarah asked.

Ken immediately looked alarmed; he had never picked up a tab for someone else's date.

"No," Joyce said, "I couldn't accept that." She put down her credit card – it was actually their joint credit card. The issue was closed.

"Have you heard anything from that girl who left her baby with you, the day we did the ferry protest?" asked Hardy, desperate to change the subject.

"Yes, I have," said Ken, "and very interesting it is too."

"Go on then." mumbled Hardy, but showing vague interest.

"Well, it turns out she is some girl. Quite different from the run-of-the-mill type you meet in most towns; she is active politically. She wants to be an MP, can you believe it, for the Tory party? She studied social history, and is very active in what she calls 'senior care'."

"That's good - we'll all be needing some of that soon."

"Yeah, dead right, she believes care for elderly people is still in the dark ages, and she uses that story she wrote as a sort of illustration."

"What like a parable?" Hardy thought he was showing real interest, but the three of them knew that his attention span was about three seconds at the moment.

"I suppose so, but she has really good ideas, even though some of them are a bit Freudian. But then again, who can argue that Freud never had logical thoughts?"

Hardy had never really studied or even read Freud, and not for the first time today lost interest in the conversation. It appeared to Ken that Hardy was dropping off again, that the spark which he had managed just two minutes ago was already being extinguished. Without warning, Ken suggested to Sarah that they up and go. He threw forty pounds on the table, saying that should cover the 'damage' they had caused. Hardy appeared a bit bewildered, wondering whether his waning interest in Ken's tale had offended him, but as they shook hands to depart, the relationship appeared intact.

And then there were two. They sat silently for about two minutes, with Hardy appearing to be only semi-conscious.

"That was a fine old to do, wasn't it?" Joyce said to Hardy.

"I not sure what's actually happened. They seem to have gone off with each other. I mean … " Hardy was rambling; he always rambled when the drink got to him.

"It does look that way. I can't believe it."

"It's bloody real that they buggered off without so much as leaving a couple of bob. Penelope made a point, you know, when I first met her, that she always went halves … was it her, or was it the other one? Probably the first one. I can't remember," drawled Hardy, and little made sense anyway to Joyce.

It struck Hardy that this was one of the most bizarre conversations and set of circumstances that he could imagine. And more than that, here was he and Joyce sitting in this nearly empty pub calmly analysing what had happened to the pair of them.

"Come on, let's pay this and go home." he said, now having got over the wave of tiredness that had washed over him.

CHAPTER THIRTEEN

A Man of Property

Hardy was sitting in the solicitor's office at Gosport Borough Council, having been told that the one relative of Bert they had been able to find was a lady called Freya Hanns. She was indeed a Salvation Army Officer, currently in Singapore. It turned out she was quite high-ranking, responsible for the corps in Malaysia as well as some of the islands off Singapore.

Ian Scarce, who had now become very familiar to Hardy, acting as the Borough's ever-dejected solicitor, had invited Hardy into his office, along with Bert's neighbour, Mrs Burgess, for a 'matter of the most importance.' Ian's deck was piled with files; there seemed to Hardy to be no order whatsoever. Wasn't that the whole point of computers – to eliminate all this paperwork?

"Freya Hanns you say?" Hardy pondered the name. "Obviously went to Singapore for hands on experience." Hardy thought that was quite good, and invited laughter from Ian Scarce and Mrs Burgess by laughing himself. It was a peculiar thing for him to do because it was one of his pet dislikes, people who laughed at their own jokes.

Hardy had originally invited Joyce to accompany him. He had felt that the events at The Deck might have softened things between them, but she had explained that his inability to remain sober had not helped either her or Penelope. Joyce was still his wife, no legal separation had taken place, and most of what had happened between them had happened in Joyce's head. It was in that context that Joyce had refused to go anywhere with Hardy. So it was Hardy and Mrs Burgess who sat before the sad-looking Ian Scarce.

"Basically, in communication with Mrs Hanns, I am satisfied that there are no further living relatives of Mr Albert Blunden. That is significant to you two, because Mrs Hanns has communicated to me that she is in no position to deal with the estate. That being the case, she feels she has no other course of action but to relinquish all claim to the estate. She has, however, made a statement that she is content to pass the matters either to myself, or to Bert's closest friends.

"I did inform her that two people probably filled that role, being the ones who were closest to him around his death, and those two people are you, Hardy, and you, Mrs Burgess. I have therefore arranged with Mrs Hanns that the full estate be transferred to you. Now there are various legal terms surrounding such transfers, and I have been able to obtain from Mrs Hanns the necessary signatures for the legal transfer of property rights to you both."

He stopped. The shock was palpable on both their faces, and it took Hardy less time than Mrs Burgess to come up with a thousand questions that the statement from the solicitor invited.

"So, can I get this straight, she wants us two to clear the house and sell it and send her the cash?" he said.

"No, anything you get from a sale or from goods, when you sign these documents for the Land Registry, goes to you both in equal part. She did indicate that it would be nice if you made a donation to the Salvation Army, which is not unreasonable."

Mrs Burgess was now comprehending more clearly.

"My goodness," she said. She hesitated. "I don't want that responsibility – I can't cope with stuff like that."

"You need to think about it, Mrs Burgess. Whilst undoubtedly there is a lot of work involved, you may – in fact you will - make financial gain from the sale of the house."

"I couldn't, and in any case I am in exactly the same situation as poor Mr Blunden was. I have no relatives to leave anything to, and besides, I am quite happy the way I am."

Hardy was listening intently to the conversation. Already he was seeing the advantage to him, even if the estate was shared with Mrs Burgess. But now she was saying she didn't want any of it. Hardy became the doer of good deeds. If it fell to him to take on this task to help with local government, then 'serve' he would.

"Look, I guess if I said no as well, you would be lumbered with a lot of work," he said to the solicitor, "and I suppose all the cash would then go to the state."

"Yes, that in a nutshell is how it works. It is a nuisance that Mrs Hanns wants nothing to do with it. I do understand it, she is working thousands of miles away and would have to come here for an indefinite period to deal with the estate of a man she hardly knew."

"Yes, Bert said he hardly knew her, and that's a bit obvious because he thought her name was Frieda."

"Yes, that complicated matters a little. But of course the Sally Army are used to that sort of thing; they have their own missing persons bureau."

Mrs Burgess had started crying. Ian Scarce (Llb Cantab) was well equipped to deal with this, producing a handkerchief from his top pocket. Fortunately it had not previously been used, its creases still crisp from ironing.

"Can I get you some water?" he asked.

"No, I'll be OK, it's all just a little overwhelming and confusing. I'm just being silly really."

Hardy's mind was working overtime (without alcohol, it did!).

"Look, if Mrs Burgess does not want to do any of this, I am quite happy to take it over. Mrs Burgess can feel free to help herself to anything she feels will give her a keepsake of Bert without any commitment whatsoever."

"Well that is a nice offer," said Ian Scarce, "but I do think Mrs Burgess should take some independent advice before agreeing to anything like that, just the same as I advised Mrs Hanns."

"I came into this office a free and unencumbered woman," she declared, "and want to leave the same way. Hardy has made a practical suggestion, and I would like to take him up on it here and now." She appeared adamant, much to the bewilderment of Ian Scarce.

"Well," said Ian Scarce, "I will place the 'minutes', if that is what you want to call them, of this meeting on record and send a copy to each of you. As soon as I have clearance from Land Registry transferring the house and contents into your name, Hardy, I will be in touch."

"Do you want me to carry on cleaning the place?" asked Mrs Burgess.

"What do you mean? Are you still going in there?

"It still gets dusty, you know."

Hardy found it a bit awkward, because the state of the place didn't indicate that much cleaning had been done.

"I didn't know you still had a key," said Ian. "No, Mrs Burgess, and will you drop the key back to me, please?" Ian replied, slightly irritated that the arrangements he had made to maintain the security of the property had been so easily compromised.

Hardy left the meeting hardly believing what was happening. He had inherited a house along with its contents. The world seemed a peculiar place, walking back home. At first he was almost skipping; the wind was still keen and he felt so alive. Now the owner of two properties and God knows what had been left in the house. Mrs Burgess wanted to walk with him, saying that she was going to the supermarket. Hardy was cautious in what he said to her, almost on edge that at any moment she could change her mind and see what she was giving up.

"I think you'd better hear this, Joyce!" Hardy shouted as he arrived back following the meeting.

He related to an evermore-incredulous Joyce the results of the meeting. Like Hardy, it took her little time to assimilate the change in circumstances that this windfall had blessed them with.

"So we are actually going to inherit his house?"

Hardy could now play a fabulous game, and he was aware he was going to enjoy it.

"We?"

There was a short silence. Joyce had forgotten herself during the telling of the tale, and had reacted as if she were still happily married to Hardy.

"Yes, we. We are, in the eyes of the law, still married, and as your lawful and wedded wife I'm entitled to as much of the estate as you are."

"Is that what you reckon? Well I can tell you, Joyce, that I may just contact my solicitors today to ask them to act before I inherit. It can also be said that I'm inheriting in return for clearing up the estate." Hardy hit back. It hadn't taken long for them to be a loggerheads again. "Look," he said, "this is stupid arguing over this now. I suppose there are still things that could go wrong between now and when the ink is dry. But we need to realise that this puts us in a position to separate properly."

Joyce realised that he was right and she had no option but to agree. Hardy retired upstairs to his part of the house, leaving Joyce full of trepidation. She sat down with a coffee to examine her feelings. Why, she was asked herself, wasn't she over the moon with glee? This was what she had wanted. Her grand plan had suddenly been made more achievable from the most unexpected source yet what she was mostly feeling was fear and perhaps sorrow. He could move in round there for real.

CHAPTER FOURTEEN
That Bloody Virus

It had been on February 6th 2020 that the BBC reported that three more cases of the Covid 19 virus, which had already ravaged some parts of the world, had been reported in the UK. Just a few weeks later, Boris Johnson announced a 'lockdown', a word with which we all were to become familiar throughout the rest of the year.

It was early in February that Hardy had signed the documents for the transfer of Bert's property. Somehow Ian Scarce had put the house into Hardy and Joyce's joint ownership. He explained to Hardy that he'd had no choice – and that being married, it was better that way anyway.

"When one of you dies, the other automatically inherits without CGT," Ian explained.

"CGT?" Hardy wished these professional people would stop using acronyms.

"Capital Gains Tax. But even that way, there are pitfalls if you have not lived in the property, I understand."

"Always the same, ain't it? What the Lord giveth with one hand, he taketh away with the other."

"You should seek professional advice on such matters," Ian concluded. "I am not qualified to help you with that."

It felt surreal to both of them as they put the key in the door. The last time Hardy had been over that threshold was the afternoon that Bert had died. He felt almost ill entering the house now, guilty at accepting this 'reward'. The first thing that hit them as the cocoa-coloured door opened was the smell. It was a combination of damp, paper, and general decay. The passageway was dark; there was a door immediately to the left which housed a lounge, unused in years it seemed.

"My God, Hardy, this is in one hell of a state," Joyce eventually said, gazing around at the general state of the place. They had entered the lounge immediately to the left of the front door.

"You're not joking."

In the weak light that came through the darkened nets surrounding the bay window, they could see a very old brown suite of furniture. They went further into the abyss. The electricity had been turned off, so the darkness seemed to reflect the general depression of the place.

"I suppose the first thing is to get the power on again," Joyce contributed.

"I don't know where the box is, usually in these older places it's in the hallway."

Hardy found the meters, and along with them the two switches which were both turned to the 'off' position. The only problem was that he couldn't reach.

"Get me a chair from the kitchen, Joyce. I need to stand on something to get this lot turned on."

He looked at the wiring: it could not have been changed since the 1950s. Leading to the fuse boxes were old rubber-clad cables, and the boxes themselves were inadequately protected by today's standards with old push-in breakers that housed a bit of fuse wire.

Joyce duly appeared with a chair and placed it in a position for him to climb on. She assisted. They were touching again, and it didn't go unnoticed by Hardy. She also had not queried what appeared to be an instruction from Hardy, she just did it! Just like the old days.

And there was light! The problem now was getting Hardy off the chair.

"I am frightened my legs are going to collapse when I get down from this height. I just don't seem to have confidence in them," he said.

"Oh, for heaven's sake," she said, "Here, hold onto my shoulder." She did not offer her hand this time.

He picked up the chair to return it to the kitchen.

"Jesus! You brought me the chair he bloody died on."

"How was I to know that was the chair? Look Hardy, it's not a shrine."

"It's disrespectful, to stand on the chair on which the man died."

The rings left by the bottle were still there on the table; all it needed was a little mood music to truly dramatise the scene.

"There's a lot of junk here – do you reckon we just get someone in to clear it?" Joyce asked.

"No I bloody don't, not until we have been through everything. We can sell furniture or even give it away to people who are willing to collect. Put it on that site, what's it called? Recycle free or something."

"Shall we go upstairs?" Joyce ventured.

"It's been a long while since you ever suggested that." He sniggered.

Joyce ignored the remark.

The stairs forked off the hallway to the right. The stair carpet had seen better days, threadbare in some places. The front bedroom offered a large dusty double bed, and a dressing table with old-fashioned scent bottles of various shapes dotted around on the surface, along with a brush that still had what was obviously a woman's hair still in it. They were both staring at it.

"Must have been his mother's."

"She's been dead for twenty years."

"Well this room hasn't been used in years, has it?"

Hardy opened one of the drawers. Bert had obviously not cleared the drawers from when his mother had used the room.

Joyce found the wardrobe full of coats and dresses.

"You know this is all quality stuff, Hardy."

There was a musty smell in the room. Some of the wallpaper was parting company with the wall and had gone brown. The bedding was good quality but full of dust: neither of them really wanted to sit on it.

"We're going to have to itemise this stuff, and I did promise Mrs Burgess that she should help herself to anything she wanted as a keepsake from Bert."

"Well I think we should have first dibs as we are doing most of the work," Joyce reasoned.

Hardy felt that was selfish. Mrs Burgess had looked after Bert and she had had been the one that found him, and she had not taken anything for it. He decided to ignore Joyce's remark and suggested they move to the back bedroom.

This was obviously Bert's bedroom. The floor had linoleum on it and the curtains were drawn. Hardy opened the curtains – not easy because they were on a plastic-covered wire. He also opened the sash windows top and bottom, risking of course a broken sash.

Both Hardy and Joyce were beginning to feel stifled by the place. There was one further room that was full to the brim with boxes.

"This is going to take weeks to sort out," Hardy said.

"Have we bitten off more than we can chew?"

"No, of course not, there is no hurry. We can do what we like when we want."

"I like the way you keep saying 'we'." This time it was Joyce that brought up the pronoun issue.

"Well you said you wanted to be involved," Hardy retorted. They were starting to bicker again, he thought. The appeal had obviously worn off now she had seen the work involved.

"You seem to be forgetting, Hardy, that we are not a couple anymore, but at the same time I am damned sure I am not missing out on any of this windfall of ours. We are still legally married, and when it comes to it, the whole estate will be divided in two, and that includes this bit." Joyce was lining up her ducks. "What this legacy does is to make it easier for both of us to separate properly. You needn't think that this bit of luck changes anything in our relationship. In fact there is no reason on earth why one of us couldn't move in here, is there?"

The remark made things seem a little bit more real, and hurt him.

"When you say 'one of us', what do you *actually* mean?"

"I'm not getting into that discussion now – we can talk about it later."

"No bloody need is there? You've already decided."

"No, Hardy, I have not."

"Well I'll tell you this, there is no way I'm living in this house; it's already giving me the creeps, and the association is not too pleasant either. That afternoon with Bert, realising it was the last few hours of his life and that I was with him, it somehow does my head in."

Joyce's response to that surprised him.

"I can understand that, and I can also understand that the place gives you the creeps – it does the same for me, but then I suspect any house that is cold, dark, slightly damp, smelly and associated with death is going to do the same."

What's going on here? Hardy wondered. She's playing with my head, he thought.

The pair had wandered downstairs again, through the kitchen and past the toilet, the toilet that had no bulb until Mrs Burgess got him one, another area of total failure for Hardy. The back door to the garden was almost opposite the toilet door, and exposed yet more work. The garden, even though now in the back end of winter, was a total mess, with strings of blackberry spreading across what had been a lawn. Blackberry was the scourge of Gosport, particularly alongside the old railway, even though the railway itself had long since disappeared.

"Just needs a strimmer really. I don't think we will venture down to that shed today."

"No, nor do I. I'm not treading over all those thorns."

Both Hardy and Joyce understood that there was a lot of work. There was also probably a lot that could be sold to add to their fortunes, but quite how that was to be achieved, neither knew.

"I suppose you could put it on these interweb sites," Hardy said.

"You mean Internet."

"Well, whatever it is. It's all the same to me, just pressing buttons and you get all sorts of weird messages."

"More than likely, given the sort of sites you visit."

"What's that meant to mean?"

"I'm not stupid, Hardy. I've known for years that you get your kicks visiting pornographic sites. Disgusting, I call it."

"Well, I had to get my 'kicks' from somewhere, didn't I?"

"Rubbish! I was still available for you, right up until a few years ago when you lost all interest in me. It was very hurtful."

Hardy had never seen the situation as hurtful to her, so this came as a surprise.

"You've never said anything about that before."

"Believe me, Hardy, there are lots of things that I have kept silent about – not worth the effort of an argument. Plus the fact that you ignore most of the things I say to you, so what's the point?"

"That's because you go on and on about the same thing. In any case, what do you mean 'a few years' ago - it must be a least ten, even more."

"Exactly ... that's probably when our marriage actually ended."

The tension between them was now spreading to Bert's house, and to Hardy it seemed inappropriate.

"Let's not argue round here please. I don't want memories of this place marred by arguments between us – the place is already full of horrible stuff for me."

"See, you are doing it again, refusing to discuss anything. You've been the same all through our married life." Hardy ignored her. "See?" said Joyce. "That is so aggressive – what they call passive aggressive."

Hardy had never thought that ignoring her was aggressive.

"Aggressive? I am trying to be absolutely the opposite. I am trying to avoid a scene round here, and disturbing Mrs

Burgess next door." They were standing in the hallway, now quite dark and cold. "Come on," said Hardy, "Let's get out of this place. I think it has the effect of making me think about our own mortality."

The next day, Hardy forced himself to spend a couple of hours at the house: Joyce came with him, yet again, determined not to miss out on anything. Her role seemed to be more 'admin', making notes of what they had found and the suggested disposal. A skip was needed, but not yet. Leave an empty skip on the street for more than one night begged for the space to be filled by those that had not paid for it.

Joyce went through the clothes and jewellery in what must have been Bert's mother's bedroom. She had started with the top drawers of the dressing table and within the first few minutes she came across a watch. It looked good – very attractive with a dark-blue face – made by a company called 'Patek Philippe'.

"Look at this," she called over to Hardy who was looking at the clothes in the wardrobe.

"Oh my God, that's a Patek Philippe."

"What's that mean?"

"They can sell for thousands of pounds, depending on the model."

"You're joking."

"No. It depends what model it is, but bring it home with you and we'll look on that internet thing."

The two of them worked together. He was throwing coats and dresses onto the bed. They wanted to start clearing stuff, and some of this could go to charity shops.

As they worked, it took him back to when they worked

together in the garage in happier days.

There was a knock on the front door. Hardy wearily trod his way downstairs to find Mrs Burgess on the doorstep.

"Hello. I couldn't help hearing that someone was in here and I just wanted to make sure it was you."

"Come in. We were just starting to clear stuff and I did say to you if you wanted anything in memory of Bert you are welcome."

"Thank you."

Joyce had parked herself at the top of the stairs and frankly could have cursed Hardy out loud. Suddenly she thought of the watch – she needed to get it into her handbag and go.

Hardy was talking to Mrs Burgess in the hall when Joyce came by in a rush.

"I need to get back home, Hardy."

"Oh, this is Joyce, she is …"

"Hello Joyce." Mrs Burgess offered a hand.

Joyce took it, but quickly continued on her 'escape'. Hardy understood that she wanted the 'watch' out of the house … but Mrs Burgess was hardly going to search her handbag.

After she'd gone, he asked Mrs Burgess if there was anything in particular that she would like from the house.

"There is," she said. "Old Mrs Blunden had a watch that I really liked."

Hardy felt his face go red; luckily they were proceeding up the dark staircase. He could not believe that this was happening. The poor woman: all she wanted was a watch and his soon-to-be ex-wife had run off with it. He decided on a neutral response.

"Well you are welcome to look for anything." Why did he feel so guilty? They were not stealing; they had merely got there before Mrs Burgess.

She seemed to know just where the watch was. She made her way straight to the small drawer in the dressing table, pushing aside some silk handkerchiefs. She turned, looking a little bewildered.

"Wonder where it is?"

"What?" Hardy played the innocent.

"Oh, not to worry, I somehow knew a watch like that would be gone. You may find it somewhere else – it was a lovely watch with a blue face. Don't know much about it apart from the fact that I really liked it."

The remark made Hardy feel even worse. If she had no idea of the value, which the skeptic in him told him that was untrue, then what Joyce had done was awful.

"Perhaps there are other things," Hardy offered.

Mrs Burgess looked at him in a very strange way, almost as if to say 'I know you two already have it'. Hardy did not offer any further commentary and Mrs Burgess returned to the other drawer. In that one was a mirrored jewellery box, marked as a present from Calais. She took it from the drawer and opened it. Hardy's eyes opened wider. There, curled up in an elastic band, was a wad of money, in old ten-pound notes. But Mrs Burgess just lifted that aside and put it on the surface of the table. There were rings, a brooch and a tie pin. There were also a pair of earrings, which to Hardy looked the business. She almost pounced on them.

"These are pretty," she said.

"Take them," he said, almost pleading.

"But it feels like stealing."

"Of course it's not. You were very good to Bert – you cared for him. You deserve this much more than we do." Hardy felt to some degree that cleared his conscience.

"I wish your wife had stayed. I would have felt better with her being here and clearing things for me. I mean legally now, everything here is yours."

"But not morally. And in actual fact it's nothing really to do with her."

"Oh, why do you say that? You should share everything as husband and wife."

Hardy hoped that Mrs Burgess was not about to embark on a course of marriage guidance.

"We are not exactly a married couple at the moment – we have separated."

"I thought you both lived together."

"Well, we are in the same property but not together, I occupy upstairs and she lives downstairs."

"That must be very difficult. I'm on my own – have been for seven years now. He died, you know. Very sad, the man suffered, he really did. Now, I'm not saying that Bert didn't suffer, but not as much as my Godfrey."

"Oh, I'm sorry."

"I do get a bit lonely. Of course Bert, bless him, didn't have much of a clue when it came to women and how they felt. Not that I wanted anything to do with him like that … you know … but even if I had, he wouldn't have had any idea. No, at our age you want action, don't you? Don't want to be messing about. No time left, to be honest."

Hardy was wondering whether he had mistaken the look she had given him. Was she giving him a sign for something else?

"I think you will be very lonely if you move in here you know," she said. It struck Hardy as a strange thing to say.

Why had she assumed that from coming not one hundred yards away he was going to be lonely, the remark made no sense at all. And he could not recall telling her of their marital arrangements. But women see through things, he reasoned.

"We don't know what we are going to do with the place yet. I have to say, although we should be very grateful, I find the house depressing."

"So do I. Of course, it may be because we both associate it with a rather pathetic old man, who frankly let the place go. It was always dark every time I came in here. But these are not bad houses. There's a lot that can be done with them. You ought to see my place."

"I would like that, it would give me an idea of what could happen in here."

"Come on then, I'll make you a cup of tea."

Hardy wondered why he had said that – he really didn't want to get involved, yet he seemed to be making a new friend.

The houses had been built around the turn of the nineteenth century. Rumour had it that they had been built for shipwrights working in the dockyard; they would have been important people and that was reflected in how spacious the houses were.

The problem today was parking, Mrs Burgess had said. The evenings were terrible, with all the workers returning between five and six o'clock, seeking a space as near to their house as possible. It caused lots of friction and even though Mrs Burgess and Bert didn't have cars, their spaces were snapped up eagerly by two-car families. The problems were even having an effect on house prices, she said.

Mrs Burgess' house was very different from Bert's, with bright wall coverings, a carpeted hall, and modern kitchen with a large window through which light poured. Hardy was impressed. Most of all, the place was warm – it had central heating, something sadly missing in the place next door.

"This is very nice," said Hardy.

"Thank you. The place next door – your place – will need some money spent on it."

That remark from Mrs Burgess struck Hardy. 'His place': the first time that he had been reminded that he owned it. He felt proud and also somewhat alarmed that he was responsible for that property now.

"Look, I can't thank you enough for not wanting to take the property."

"Oh goodness, I didn't want it. Just a shame that the one thing I did want is missing, and I cannot think for the life of me where it would have gone. I mean the only person that's been in there is that solicitor fellow from the town hall, and I can't imagine him rifling through the drawers."

Hardy wondered if he was blushing again. He was cross with Joyce; this was beginning to feel extremely mean, and it also felt like Mrs Burgess knew exactly where the watch had gone. It struck him that she might know a lot more about what was in that house than he did.

"Did you know where it was, this watch?" Hardy found himself asking.

"Oh, yes, I put it in the old lady's drawer just after I found Bert. I put it in there for security. You see, I had no idea who was going to poke around in the place. I just didn't want someone seeing it and just picking it up. I think Bert must have got it out months ago and just left it on the dressing table."

Hardy was dying to ask why she felt it necessary to go upstairs and into the front bedroom when Bert was slumped dead over the table in the kitchen.

The kettle boiled and she made a pot of tea.

"Here, let me show you upstairs while the tea is brewing."

The stairs were carpeted and the whole house was extremely clean and tidy. The bathroom smelt of air freshener and her bedroom window was open, giving air to the place. Her bedroom was large and uncluttered: given the size compared with modern homes, the space could be split in half and still provide two good sized bedrooms.

Mrs Burgess sat on the end of the bed.

"My hubby and I had lots of fun in this room." She paused, "I miss that, you know. I mean even in his agony, he still looked after my needs."

Hardy struggled for a neutral reply.

"Yes, I am sure you did, and it's great to have memories," he said.

"Don't you miss female company? Or are you what they call nowadays still friends with benefits?"

The million-dollar question, the entrapment question, he thought. What should he say?

"Oh God no, we cannot be described even as friends now. Well, we haven't been friends as such for years, and things are very awkward with her downstairs."

"To be honest I have never heard of anything like your situation. She must be desperate to be alone I guess, but that can all change now can't it?"

"I suppose it can."

She hesitated.

"But you don't want it to, do you?"

Why were females so insightful? Here was another one that seemed to know his mind better than he did.

"Do you know, Mrs Burgess, I don't really know."

There was about a ten second silence that seemed much

longer, then she said: "Perhaps you should sample other fruits? May put your mind in a different place."

Hardy felt very uncomfortable, particularly as he did not fancy Mrs Burgess at all. He knew that, because if he had fancied her, Joyce would not have left, even with the state of their relationship as it was. Joyce seemed to know when there were sparks between him and any other female.

"I have tried online dating," he said, moving towards the door. "But look, I really must get going now – I have an appointment at lunchtime with the solicitor." A lie, but a useful one.

"Will you not have time for tea now?"

"No thank you, I have to go back home first to pick up some documents."

Hardy beat a hasty retreat, thinking that he had handled things quite well. He had not been rude and felt that perhaps now he had put her right, they could be good friends in the future. As he walked home, he realised that he felt flattered that she had 'tried it on' with him – it had boosted his confidence. But why? He was a stupid old man with few masculine attributes, perhaps after all he had misinterpreted the whole thing. But thinking about it, what he had now was money.

CHAPTER FIFTEEN

'You Must Stay at Home'

In normal circumstances Hardy and Joyce would be living different lives, but normal circumstances had been suddenly suspended. Death and illness appeared in the shape of Covid 19 to pretty much every member of society in every nation of the earth. It did not discriminate: Prime Ministers, Royals, those on benefits, and even terrorists were all in the same boat for once.

"Stay at home, do not go out unless you have to for medical appointments, exercise or food shopping." That's what the blond Prime Minister said in his televised address to the nation.

Hardy stood and shouted down the stairs.

"Did you hear that?"

"What?"

"The Prime Minister."

"What about him?"

"Christ, you always miss the important things in life, don't you? He is stopping us going out."

It was obvious that Joyce had been watching some tripe on the 'Drama' or 'Yesterday' TV channels.

"He's closing all shops, offices, factories, schools. No-one is allowed out."

"He can't just say we can't go out – what about shopping? And why?"

Hardy made his way downstairs. "Put it on," he said. "It's on the BBC, they are still discussing it."

"Oh, the BBC, they will be exaggerating all over the place, gloom and doom."

She did, however, turn over the channel, and of course there was the usual crew of four or five people sitting round a table in the studio, gloom-mongering. Hardy stood behind her chair watching the unfolding disaster on TV. He could smell that familiar yet provocative scent of her expensive Chanel perfume. It always brought back memories of days much more pleasant.

"Bloody hell," she eventually said. She immediately saw the complication here with their relationship …. and the solution. "You could move round there in the morning," she said, out of the blue.

"No, *you* could move round there in the morning."

"You're the one it was left to."

"Oh funny that, isn't it? Yesterday it was 'our' house, but today it is suddenly mine. It was transferred to both of us."

There was a few seconds of silence.

"Why don't you want to go and live there?" she asked eventually.

"Come on, probably the same reasons you don't. It's cold, damp, smells and it's in one hell of a state. It has memories for me as well."

"All that can be fixed."

"Yes, of course it can, but not tonight, and it looks like it won't be able to be fixed for the foreseeable future."

"Look Hardy, I don't want this situation going on and on. Once this Covid business is over, we have to come up with a plan to separate properly."

Hardy thought what a bitch she was. She could have just left things. She knew full well that he would not want to live round there in the condition the place was. She also had no intention of moving out. This Covid crisis had bought him more time. This was going to be really interesting, he thought: neither of them would be going out to meet anyone else. They were allowed to shop for essential provisions, but no other shops would be open, no restaurants, no pubs, no DIY shops, nothing. Apparently even churches were shutting.

"That's a real infringement of civil liberties, he can't just do that," Joyce complained.

"Well, he has. Puts an end to our dating for a while."

"Don't think we were doing very well with it anyway. Have you heard from that woman since she and David went off together?"

"No, have you heard from him?"

"No, shame really, because he was a nice man."

"And Penelope was a nice woman. It was nice to be with someone who was not criticising me all the time."

"Well, she doesn't know you that well yet, does she? She hasn't had to put up with years of failure, moaning and boredom."

Hardy decided to ignore the remark, which indicated there had been no change to his strategy that had lasted as many years as he could recall.

The pandemic kept them indoors: they were particularly upset by the closure of the church, because church was just about the only time either of them ever spoke to anyone else. The TV news was alarming and depressive, and the weather seemed to reflect the mood of the country as well. A fortnight into this and Joyce was talking to Hardy on a daily basis.

Joyce had thought hard during this enforced isolation. In real terms, the lockdown meant very little to them apart from Sundays. Hardy was now shopping for both of them; he would queue outside Morrisons and be allowed in only when one person came out. That was their little bit towards the national effort. Hardy would go there early on a Monday morning, saying it avoided what he called the 'social housing' people who would not be getting up early because the kids were not at school. Their shopping list was bizarre because he bought two of everything. He even felt he should explain to the checkout lady.

"I'm shopping for my 'bubble'," he said … which was not a lie. He was surprised at how disciplined most shoppers were. They were keeping apart. There actually seemed to be fear in the air, fear of the terrible death that this Covid thing seemed to inflict. There was always an exception, of course: one woman, as if she had no idea what was going on, had no mask on and took no notice of distancing. She lost her temper and stormed out after various comments. Hardy supposed she was going to try her luck in some other store.

There were so many different byproducts of the lockdown. Hardy and Joyce's next-door-neighbour Sandra, a woman in her early thirties whose husband was in the Royal Navy, suddenly acquired a puppy. She had said to Joyce over the garden fence that she couldn't stand not going out to work – she needed something. So the puppy was the 'something'. Even Hardy admitted that it was cute.

"What is it?" he asked.

"A cockapoo," she told him, over the garden wall. "They are a spaniel and a poodle cross."

Hardy remembered when he was a child and the family had had a Cocker Spaniel for a short time. But it had had to go: it was mad. The energy had been non-stop and it was also aggressive. Hardy wondered what the effect of mixing a poodle into that was going to be. The puppy had spaniel ears, and was a rich light brown in colour. And it was certainly lively.

"To be fair, it hasn't made much noise. I don't think I have even heard it bark yet," Hardy said to Joyce.

"I have, it has a very high-pitched yap." Joyce was obviously not a fan of any animal. Sometimes Hardy wondered what actually did interest her. But the way Joyce voiced the comment was almost offensive.

It wasn't long before Sandra was sounding a bit desperate. She had not really examined the logistics of dog owning. She was obviously getting fed up with having to take the animal out twice a day.

"I don't suppose you would help by taking the dog out?" she asked Hardy. "You are allowed to do that – exercise a pet." Hardy wondered if Sandra thought she was doing them a favour by getting them out of the house for a lawful reason

Hardy could not cope with desperate women. Of course he would take the dog out. Sandra was very conscientious: she arranged to tie the dog to their gate post and Hardy would pick it up from there. At least it got him out, and he decided to take it over to Walpole Park, a huge area with few trees. The park went down to Haslar Creek, but the view was slightly spoilt by two ugly gasometers. From the park side you could see the old naval gunboat yard and the submariners' escape tower in what was HMS Dolphin, the submarine base for the south coast. Like so many other properties in Gosport, the MoD neither wanted it nor wanted to dispose of it.

Hardy stood there surveying the scene. He was reluctant to let the dog off the lead. It was such a lively little thing, and had both pulled and run around on the lead in the short walk over to the park. He had made the occasional attempt at training the little mite, when the puppy pulled too hard on the lead, and he had sternly said 'Heel! Heel!'. Hardy knew that when the dog actually did what it was meant to do you needed to make a fuss and tell him that he was a good boy. The routine reminded him of his marriage really – he could remember the days when he had been a 'good boy'.

But now the dog had wrapped the lead around Hardy's leg. He was aware that he was just standing there staring at the muddy bottom of the creek, and this was not the dog's idea of fun. Hardy decided to take the risk and let it off the lead.

"Joyce! Joyce! Hello. Look, what's the bleeding dog's name?" he shouted into his mobile phone.

"You haven't let it off the lead, have you?"

"Just find out the bloody name." Hardy was losing his temper.

"You have, haven't you?"

"Its name – now!" he shouted.

"Sometimes I wonder about you. Good job you actually had your mobile on you."

Why couldn't she just tell him the dog's name? Then it became clear.

"I'll ring the door bell and ask."

"Just hurry, will you? The thing looks like it's finding the mud in the creek very interesting."

Joyce said she would ring him back, but was secretly enjoying Hardy's situation. There was no guarantee that the dog would respond to its name anyway. It was still very young and probably hadn't been trained to come back when its name was called.

Hardy was rushing (strolling, by anybody else's measure) towards the creek. There was another woman over there with an Alsatian.

His mobile phone rang, the ring tone, 'Rule Britannia' seeming unusually loud in the surroundings.

"It's 'Buster'."

"Thanks."

By now Buster had engaged in play with the Alsatian. It seemed to be enjoying itself, but Hardy was more concerned about getting it back safely on the lead. He got closer to the owner of the Alsatian.

"Aren't they having a great time?" The owner greeted Hardy.

"Yes, they appear to be." he drawled, now wondering whether this whole thing was such a good idea.

"He's lovely, how old is he?" she asked.

He looked at her. She was in her early fifties and wearing an anorak of grey and blue, with jeans and grey wellington boots. She wore a bobble hat that was green, and which failed to match the otherwise faultless colour scheme.

"I think he's about four months. It's not my dog, I'm just taking it for a walk for our neighbour."

"How kind, what a nice thing to do."

"Well, to be honest it gets me out as well, but I'm now finding this a bit stressful. I shouldn't have let him off the lead."

"I shouldn't worry, he's playing with Alice. When she comes back, he will."

Hardy was less certain. The two dogs were now seriously close to the banks of the creek. The bank was only three or four feet, and easily negotiated by a dog, but not him.

"Oh God!" exclaimed Hardy.

The two dogs had done exactly what he did not want to happen. Both had now disappeared from sight into the creek, which contained half sea and half mud and the occasional tyre or supermarket trolley. The creek accepted surface water from a sewer at the top end, a pipe large enough for any dog to run up.

"They will love it down there," said the woman. Hardy failed to share that view. They both walked over to the edge. Hardy was first to note that Buster was learning about life and the sea. The sea where, if you were so inclined, you could board a boat in Haslar creek and get all the way to New York.

Alice, much more used to the scene than Buster, continued to run around while Buster put a tentative paw into the water, not sure of this big puddle, Buster decided to seek the advice of Alice by doing a bit more sniffing.

"Alice, back you come luv!" shouted the woman.

Alice looked back at her owner, as much as to say 'who are you kidding? I like it down here.' She went further up the creek. It was very muddy there as water was still trickling out of the sewer. It was, of course, meant to be fresh surface water, but most in Gosport were aware that 'fresh' was sometimes not quite the adjective that should be used. Buster followed and started to sink into the mud.

"Bloody hell, can't we get them back? Buster!" Surprisingly, Buster did look up, but in common with Alice, these two dogs were going to call the shots.

"Never get cross with them, they pick that up and then you stand no chance of getting them back," she explained to Hardy.

"What other chances do you have then?"

"Food. There is hardly an animal on the planet that does not respond to food, and you know that includes humans if they are hungry enough."

Hardy had no food on him, or nothing that the dog would respond to. The only thing he could find was a half-used packet of Polo mints that showed signs of age. The top one could be described as grubby. However, the woman had dog biscuits on her, which she now brandished in the air, calling Alice yet again, and added Buster to the list for good measure. Both dogs responded. Alice jumped in an attempt to get the biscuit, but the woman was up to that, lifting her arm just enough for Alice to fail in the attempt.

"Sit! Sit!" she commanded. Hardy actually wondered whether he was meant to respond as well. Alice and Buster sat.

"I would get the lead on Buster now," she suggested.

Hardy found it difficult to bend down to the collar, but upon managing it, he found himself very close to the woman's jean-covered crotch.

The dreadful thing was that Hardy could not get back up without holding onto her anorak, and he knew that nowadays that was an invasion of private space. The woman was indifferent, and Hardy was doubly relieved: he hadn't offended her and he had recaptured his charge.

"There, I told you not to worry. Now I must give him a bit of this biscuit otherwise it doesn't work next time." She proceeded to give Buster half.

"Look, thanks, I don't even know your name. I'm Hardy."

"Hi, nice to meet you. I'm Olivia. I'm always over here at this time."

Hardy consulted his watch and made a mental note of the time.

"I'd better get back, but I may see you tomorrow if they allow me out again."

"Look forward to it."

Hardy took his leave, and headed back to Stoke Road. It went through his head: she said it was nice to meet me. She looked forward to next time!

Buster was only slightly less energetic that he had been in his trip over, and was still pulling. Hardy took the opportunity to train Buster a bit and he went into the same routine of commanding the dog to heel. This time Buster actually did heel for a few seconds and was duly awarded with a 'good boy'. The only problem was that he looked a completely different animal to the one that had been collected from the gatepost. He was wet and muddy, and some was beginning to cake on the longer parts of his coat. The other thing that Hardy noticed was that there was a sewage-like smell coming from Buster.

"God, Buster, you are a mess. And you stink."

Buster looked up at him, those appealing eyes taking away any anger that Hardy might otherwise have had.

Joyce was not happy with Hardy bringing the dog back to their home.

"I can't take him back like this – we need to clean him off a bit."

"And how are you going to do that?"

Buster did a dog shake. The shake that gets rid of things he doesn't want and spreads it all over wallpaper and floors. No longer Buster's problem, but very much the problem of a human trying to keep their own kennel clean and tidy.

Hardy phoned Sandra.

"He's a bit dirty and damp at the moment – he went

down the creek."

"He does that – just put him back at the front door. He can dry off in the garden. That's what we always do."

"I was so worried about what you would say, returning Buster in a mess. Anyway, if this is normal, I'm quite happy to take him again tomorrow, around the same time."

"That's great, a really big help. My husband is home now and has to isolate before he joins his ship, and then has to pass some tests."

"Well, providing it's helping, I'll pick Buster up tomorrow."

"I'll leave him tied to the gate just the same as today."

Buster was waiting for him, but the weather was bad; it was raining and windy and nowhere near as pleasant as the day before. Hardy was regretting the rash offer, and remembered that old saying, 'a dog is for life not just for Christmas.'

Would Olivia be there in this weather?

Buster was still pulling but had been so pleased to see Hardy, his tail going ten to the dozen, that it lifted Hardy's heart. This was a 'being' that was giving unconditional love, or was it conditional on a walk? He could not see the creek until he had crossed the relief road. But sure enough, there was a figure he could make out in the rain, and sure enough a four-legged friend running around after a pointless ball. She wore the same kit, but this time her jeans were soaked.

"Hi Olivia, not a great idea this, is it?"

"Goes with the territory I am afraid. When you have a dog, you can't pick and choose when you go out."

The rain was now driving in at them. It ran down Hardy's nose, and he was not sure whether it was rain or whether it was a runny nose, but he constantly needed to wipe it with his gloved hand.

Olivia offered a rather attractive alternative.

"Why don't we go back to my place? The two dogs could play in the garden and we could have a cup of tea."

She recovered Alice without a problem, so much so that Hardy wondered if the dogs could speak, that they also felt this was beyond what could be considered pleasurable. Olivia, it transpired, did not live that far away from Joyce and Hardy. How come he had not seen her before? Perhaps he had, but had never taken any notice her.

The house was nicely furnished but smelt of dog. They ushered the dogs to the back door. The garden was lawned, with burnt-out bits that Alice had obviously destroyed by her urine.

"Take your coat off and make yourself comfortable."

"This is very nice of you," he said, "particularly as you hardly know me."

"But I do, Hardy. I have seen Buster about before, he is from next door to you and you live on this road, so it's pretty safe I would guess."

She was wearing a green jumper under her coat; it was a polo neck and went right up to her chin. What it also did for Hardy was to give him a clue as to her figure, which was 'ample'.

"Tea or coffee?" she asked. Hardy elected for coffee. "So, we are technically breaking the law. Do you have a bubble?"

Hardy didn't know what she meant at first, then realised that all mixing was banned. You could have one person in a bubble with you but outside of that no one was allowed in somebody else's house.

"No," he eventually got out.

"That's OK then, nor have I. So if there is any query, we can say you are visiting me on welfare grounds to make sure I am OK. Are you married, incidentally?"

That seemed very forward. But then the lesson of the last few months for Hardy had been that women these days were as forward as men. Hardy looked out of the bay window; while he couldn't actually see his own house because of the angle, he realised he was only a few yards away. Somehow that felt weird, almost taboo. This is stupid he thought, he was reading much more into this than there possibly could be.

"Yes, but we don't live together." That was now his stock answer, but of course it always drew more questions.

"Never simple is it? I'm divorced, but it was quite messy really."

"How long have you been divorced?"

"About four years, but he didn't move out until about a year ago. I had to get a court order in the end." Hardy thought he was about to hear another tale of woe, but she closed it. "I don't want to talk about that part, it is still too painful."

"I understand. Everyone tells me that divorce isn't easy. I think it has something to do with the adversarial procedures that we have in this country. Perhaps if the courts were kinder and people coached a bit better as to what to expect, then the whole system would be less painful."

"Mason and I went to no end of counselling sessions," she said. "They always wanted to talk about your sex life or lack of it. They look for problems where there aren't any, and then miss the big issue where there is one."

"We never went to anything like that, although my wife did go and see the vicar. That was largely unhelpful. Were there any children involved?"

"Yes, they are all grown now though. I have three daughters and one son. Our son Robert is the youngest, and he joined the Royal Navy as an Officer Cadet just before we broke up. He's a Sub Lieutenant now."

"You must be proud."

"Yes, we both are, but the divorce affects all of them. The girls sided with their dad, but Robert stayed on the fence, not wanting really to get involved. One of the girls went to University down in Exeter, and the other one is cabin crew for British Airways. Of course she's been furloughed because there are no commercial flights taking off from the UK, and other nations are pretty much the same. Some of the pilots have even been laid off – I mean pilots, for heaven's sake!"

"This is really beginning to affect all of us, isn't it?"

"Yes it is."

"So what about the other one?" Hardy asked realising that she had told him about one boy and two girls, there was one missing.

"Truth is, I don't know what she is doing. She went to Amsterdam last year, and apart from a phone call every so often to let us know she is alive, I have very little clue about her life. Last I heard was that she was working as a PA to some guy that owned a few cargo ships. She's still got a bedroom here, and this place is used as her postal address, but apart from official stuff, nothing else comes."

"So what's the one in University doing now?"

"She's shacked up with her boyfriend down there. Course, they're not allowed to travel home either. She's good though; she does ring me to check how I am, and she also keeps me up to date with her dad's situation."

"Can I ask where her dad is now?"

"Well apparently he is in Bed and Breakfast out at Stubbington. It's not ideal: he's with an older couple but the wife is an alcoholic and gets rat-arsed pretty much every day, according to Kate – sorry, that's my daughter."

"Is he working?"

"He took early retirement during the divorce. Said he wasn't working for a pension for me to take half of it. He was very bitter at that point."

"I'm getting the impression that he didn't want to split up." Hardy was looking for an answer even though it wasn't a question.

"No, he didn't, and it took me a long time to realise that we were in fact not 'together' any more. He'd had the odd fling, saying it meant nothing. It probably didn't, but it's never one thing, is it? It's always an accumulation of things that make you realise that it's over. I didn't help, I know that. I had an affair that was really just for revenge. I mean, what is it they say? 'Reciprocation is a potent aspect of human behaviour.'"

Hardy looked puzzled. 'Where did you get that from?'

'It was in a book I was reading last night and I felt it sounded good. Anyway, it just goes down and down from there. You realise that other people are all trying to plough a path through what is really quite a shitty life."

"Did he have to leave your house in the end? I mean was that part of the court stuff?"

"No, the court has ordered a sale – or for one of us to buy the other out - but that's useless. You split this in two and you've got nothing much of any value. Neither of us would get a mortgage now."

"So how was the decision made as to who was going to move out?"

"It wasn't. He got violent with me, so at the moment he

is under a court order not to molest me."

"Could you not have moved out? I mean, what do the courts say in situations like this where you can't agree?" Hardy was by now genuinely interested.

"No, where there are no underage children involved, they leave it to the parties to sort out. In our case my solicitor applied for what's known as a delaying order. But at the end of the day, they probably will order that the house be sold and all assets split between us. I may have a chance to stay it on the grounds of his unreasonable behaviour, but that's highly unlikely."

Hardy was silent. Surely Joyce had not thought all this through.

"We – you may find this strange – we live in the same house still. I live upstairs and she lives down."

"That sounds a good solution, as long as you can work out suitable living arrangements."

Hardy wished that Joyce was here to hear that. Debbie continued:

"I won't pretend that this has been easy. The girls make their views clear every so often. And I don't have an answer to them when they accuse me of engineering the situation to where it is now. Mason took to drink during the divorce – it changed him into somebody I didn't recognise."

"But you didn't like the man you did recognise, did you?"

"Oh crikey, don't you start as well! The children think we should have just stumbled on, but I thought there would be a new life out there. There isn't."

Hardy understood: she was preaching to the converted.

They drank their coffee in silence.

"My God, these jeans are soaking," she suddenly said. "Would you excuse me for just a moment? I need to get out of them and put something else on."

Hardy's mind went wild. This was the 'I need to slip into something more comfortable' syndrome. She was lonely and in Hardy's mind she was desperate for it. He fully expected a half-clad Olivia to reappear, but in the meantime it gave him chance to explore his current environment a little more. The room's scheme of red and grey gave a sense of warmth and homeliness and a gas fire was pumping out heat. There were pictures on the wall – one looked like an original – showing a view of the coast with a large lighthouse. He thought it looked rather amateurish. The light wooden sideboard hosted the normal supply of family photographs, all of them posed as students except for the young man in the naval midshipman's uniform passing out of Dartmouth.

He heard movement upstairs, sending his mind racing again as to what she was changing into. He wasn't sure why he was getting excited: he couldn't say he really fancied her. She was plain, he thought, with no features that tripped his switch, but the idea of a woman provoking him always excited him. Now he could hear her coming down the stairs, so he distracted himself by taking a gulp of the boiling hot coffee. There she was, in the doorway. She had replaced the jumper and jeans for a dress: a black dress with yellow flowers on it. It was not a posh dress, in fact in looked more like something you would wear in the summer. She had combed her grey-blonde hair.

"That's better," she said.

Hardy smiled. "How long have you lived here?" he asked.

"In Gosport all my life, but in this house about twenty-four years. Brought the children up here, so it's home for them as well."

"Long time. Was your husband in the navy?"

"Yes, but he only ended as a Chief Petty Officer, not like my son who is commissioned." Hardy noted the resentment there. "We had a good time though," she said. "I went to Gibraltar with him, smashing time. When I first met him, he wasn't even a killick then."

"A killick?"

"It's slang for a leading hand."

"I have learnt no end of things round here today."

Did he detect that her legs were getting further apart?

"I wonder if the dogs are OK?" she said, changing the subject.

"They were alright when you went up to change."

Hardy got the impression that she was staring at him. He found himself looking around the room in order avoid his eyes meeting hers. Why? he thought. Why do I not want eye contact? He could not understand it.

He had not mentioned that he was the owner of two houses … along with Joyce. In fact he had not said much about himself at all. Perhaps that was good thing, and yet he seemed to know so much about her. There was a short silence in the conversation, the sort of silence where lots of things can be said. He did eventually move his gaze over to her, and she was now taking some of the coffee, so eye contact was minimal. His eyes went to her legs again. Yes, they had parted even further, and she had pulled her dress up. Hardy had to admit that she had a nice set of pins.

She twisted round to put her cup on the table, and the dress rose a good three inches further up her thighs; she also allowed her legs to 'balance' her, which included a further parting of the way. Hardy found himself quite nervous, now convinced that he was meant to initiate some action here. He did.

"Right, it's time I was going."

As he gathered the dog, and rushed back through the house to the front door, Olivia had a confused expression on her face.

"Thank you for this morning, I really enjoyed it," he eventually said, standing at the front door. He felt a bit safer there.

"I will always be over the park at about the same time," she said as a farewell.

CHAPTER SIXTEEN
Absurd Conversations

"This is stupid," Hardy eventually said to Joyce, while unpacking the groceries. "Let's stop this nonsense, even if only for the duration of this Covid crisis. We should share stuff, because we're both spending a fortune at the moment."

Joyce agreed it made sense, but this really wasn't going the way she wanted, with more and more integration between the pair of them. The pandemic was pushing them closer together again.

The following Monday, Hardy's arrival at Morrisons was another eye-opener. Many of the shelves had been stripped and in particular the toilet roll shelves were almost empty. He grabbed a packet of three, because that was all there was, and this packet was of such luxury he would not have given it houseroom prior to this epidemic. He reasoned that perhaps he had always masochistically denied himself such comfort. He was suddenly taken back to the era of IZAL, which was more like greaseproof paper and absorbed very little. Why he was thinking such things bewildered him, but it did give him something to think about in the queue. He'd had to queue to get into the shop: others in the queue had told him it was worse over at ASDA.

Away from Morrisons' car park, Hardy became aware of the silence. There was hardly a vehicle on the road. He could hear birds and the wind; in a peculiar sort of way he became slightly scared. This was indeed a new experience, one which he and probably everyone else was not used to.

It was almost a relief to see another car; it was as if the world had died. People were nowhere to be seen except in the store. People were panicking, the thought of no food playing uppermost in the mind..

"Did you get what I wanted?" asked Joyce on his return.

"No, I bloody didn't. You are frankly lucky to get anything. There are empty shelves all over the place." He placed two bags on the table, making a suffering noise in doing so. "That's done my shoulders in, carrying them."

"Why didn't you take the car?"

"I did, but couldn't get the car through the bleeding front door, could I?"

"No need to swear, I was only asking."

"I am trying to get through to you that it was far from a pleasant experience, and not one I am looking forward to repeating."

Joyce was unloading the bags, inspecting everything as it came out.

"Why on earth did you get these toilet rolls? There's only three here and you can get a packet of twelve for the same price as these."

"I am obviously not making this clear – the shelves are empty; you have to queue to get in. I had to wear a mask, which fogged up my glasses and I could not reach stuff that was on the lower shelf. All in all, totally horrible."

Joyce looked at him. She had never noticed before, but he seemed to look old today.

He went to sit down.

"Don't make yourself at home down here," she said.

"For God's sake, I just want to sit down for a minute." He sounded a little breathless. He groaned. "I ache all over today, and my knee – my right one – is particularly painful today. Now my shoulders ache. I'm falling to bits."

"Hardy, for heaven's sake, it's called getting old. I get aches and pains, but they are here today and gone tomorrow."

"Yeah, of course, but today I feel quite down."

"What are we doing with the potatoes – are we just sharing them out?"

"Yeah, guess so. Give me a jug of milk, will you?"

Hardy was right: this was appearing a little silly, but Joyce knew that if she relented on this arrangement she would soon find herself back in the position prior to separation, and that she did not want.

"Yes, of course." She was almost polite. "Do you want a cup of tea?"

"I could murder one."

Hardy stayed for about an hour. She had switched on Radio Four, where the last strains of the 'Today' programme were being played out. They were talking of nothing but this damned Covid 19.

"It can finish the likes of us, Joyce, if we catch it," said Hardy mournfully.

"It's a lung infection, isn't it?"

"Not really sure, but they are frightened that the number of cases will overload the NHS, not that they aren't overloaded already. I suppose this would be a new overload, one which the government would not be responsible for. So in a way, this sort of thing is a dream for them."

Whatever else Joyce perceived to be wrong with Hardy, lack of insight was not one of his faults. He did seem to understand politics, which always amazed her because he seemed to understand little else about life.

"The other thing is that I reckon this virus is a man-made thing," he said. "Do you remember that guy that used to use our garage? The one that worked for some defence company. He always said that the ideal weapon is one that behaves inconsistently and doesn't kill everyone, so governments are obliged to protect the population – and that that kills off economic activity. Well, here it is."

"Yes, but they think it has come from a 'wet market' in China, whatever that is."

"They're not going to tell you the truth, are they? The population of the world would be up in arms– there would be more than just an epidemic to sort out, there would bound to be calls for military action, or a boycott of their goods, and no one wants that."

"On the other hand, it could just be an accident that they won't admit to," said Joyce.

Hardy seemed to drift off. He had his cup of tea and was as comfortable as he was going to get today. Joyce nudged him.

"Do you want a biscuit?"

"I won't say no."

Joyce attacked a new packet of shortbreads. She could not pull the cellophane wrapping apart from one end, so she tried the other. The packaging would still not yield to her desperate tugging. She noticed a red line going round the wrapping and an arrow. She fiddled with the 'thin red line' but could not find the beginning or end of the damned thing.

"For Pete's sake, Joyce, give it here."

She did. Hardy now wrestled with the same end that he hoped Joyce had weakened but to no avail. He claimed that Joyce had made it slippery and he could not get a grip, so he attacked the other end. Same thing, and to be sure his sausage-like fingers could be of no assistance with the 'thin red line'.

"Give it back here."

Joyce took a knife to the packet, stabbing the tube with gusto. That worked. At last, the   forbidden fruit was available to both of them. Hardy promptly dipped the shortbread in his tea. Joyce hated that but had learned to live with it provided he washed up the cup. There always seemed to be a residue of biscuit in the bottom - and sometimes a half a biscuit when he had mis-timed the dunking process. Hardy had explained to her years ago that he had picked up the habit from his mother and her friends who every Thursday would meet for some women's 'do'. They all dunked and he grew to like it, particularly with Lincoln biscuits that had little lumps all over them.

"You can't get them nowadays, can you?" Hardy said, not realising that Joyce had no idea what he was talking about.

"Can't get what?"

"Lincoln biscuits."

"Who was talking about Lincoln biscuits?" Joyce was wondering whether she had missed something.

"I was just thinking about them."

"It's going to be really funny not going to church this morning," said Joyce on Sunday.

"Yeah, and there's nowhere else to go either."

"You regard it as a social occasion, don't you?" she said. "It's not meant to be – it's an act of worship."

Hardy gave her one of his uncomprehending stares. "What? You use it as a networking organisation. Don't give me that rubbish about you missing an act of worship."

"Well, yet again, confirmation that you don't really know me after all these years. You have never once talked to me about my faith. I'm like the Queen – I don't make a fuss, I just find enormous strength in my faith."

"I've heard it all now – my wife is like the Queen! Oh my God, we'll have the bloody Royal Marine band outside in a minute, and a red carpet."

She ignored him. She could take that rubbish: he had done it all their married life.

Without thinking, she had put a dress on. After all, it was Sunday morning and she always wore a dress on Sunday morning.

Hardy had come downstairs again. Why, he didn't really know. He was at a loose end, there was nothing on the television and he could not be bothered to go out to the garden which was just beginning to burst into life, with spring just around the corner. The news on the television was depressing, with cases of Covid rising dramatically, and worst of all was the death rate. They were both alarmed to find out that they were considered vulnerable because of their age, and should be very careful. Indeed, lots of people were being told to 'shield', which meant they could not go out at all: shopping and medicines had to be delivered or bought by good friends and helpers. These volunteers seemed to be springing up everywhere, and Hardy found it reassuring that there was still some spirit in the country of pulling together.

"What you standing there for?" Joyce eventually asked him.

"I don't really know. What you going to do with yourself this morning? And this afternoon, come to that?"

Instead of saying 'none of your business, she said: "Don't really know at the moment. What are you doing?"

"Don't know. We are allowed to exercise, so I thought I might go for a walk down the front."

"It's going to be freezing down there."

Hardy had to work out in his head whether she had intended joining him on the walk. She normally could not be bothered in the slightest if he was 'freezing his nuts off'.

"I can't stand just walking anyway. For me, there has to be a purpose to it– shopping or going to meet someone," she said.

"I know what you mean, and the other thing is I suppose there will be nothing much happening in the Harbour."

"Is the Gosport Ferry still running?"

"Don't know. I mean, it carried on all through the war, didn't it?"

"Yes it did, and did you know when the company wanted to protect their captains on the bridge from falling debris by putting a roof on it, but they had to take it off because the War Office wanted the metal?"

"I did read about that," said Hardy.

Joyce was consulting her tablet.

"It's running a single service with passenger numbers seriously down. They have to wear masks on the pontoons and ferry and be socially distanced."

"Do you know what, I don't know whether I would even want to be on the thing in those austere conditions," said Hardy. "It's horrible."

Days came and went. There was little difference between Monday and Sunday; Tuesdays were marked by Joyce watching a favourite drama series on television. One day was set aside for changing the bedlinen, and they made one wash out of it. Television was doing its level best to depress the nation more than anything else, with hour-after-hour coverage of the pandemic.

"Why don't we play a game of Scrabble – take our minds off everything for a while?"

"Scrabble? We haven't played Scrabble for years." he exclaimed.

"Well there's lot' of things we haven't done for years, isn't there? I just thought a game of something might break this boredom. I'm fed up with the telly, and now they can't seem to make any new programmes it's all repeats."

"Where is it then?" Hardy eventually asked.

The game was buried in a sideboard that had remained in the same place it had been for years. Rescuing it from the depths of the sideboard reminded Hardy of the times they had played in the past.

Joyce, he always said, was a hoarder. She showed that in so much as she would keep the 'z' or 'q' until she could get maximum points with them. Hardy needed instant gratification and got them out as soon as one appeared in his letters. She was the same with an 's'. She always held one back in reserve, whereas Hardy, would use it as soon as possible to make plural a previously singular word.

He took pride in creating words that either opened the board up, or words that showed his erudition. Joyce would scoff at such confidence, but would still score the points and invariably wipe the floor with him. Hardy sometimes had fun, putting down words that he knew would offend her., just to get a reaction. But he had worked out that this 'game' told him so much about Joyce, and there again, it must have told Joyce so much about him.

"Oink is not a word." he argued.

"It is. It's the noise a pig makes."

Hardy immediately followed with 'poo'.

"Here we go, just two words and you bring the board down to something that looks like kids are playing the game."

"It's in the dictionary, so it counts."

"So it may be, but that's not the point. You only put down words like that to wind me up. Why can't you just be civil and normal like other men?"

"You don't know any other men, so how can you say that?"

Joyce decided to ignore that one, and proceeded with her next word, which proved difficult with such short words occupying the middle like that.

Going back years, Hardy remembered one of his better jokes that annoyed her, but made the other two players laugh. Joyce had got up saying she needed to use the toilet, but was so secretive about her letters that she took her tiles to the toilet with her, so nobody would know what she had. When she returned she noticed that she only had six letters,

"I must had dropped one." she said.

Hardy, quick as lightning said, "Perhaps you've left a 'P' in the pan."

Joyce was not a fan of this type of 'toilet' humour, but even she had to smile at that, before she decided to round on him.

"Well if I have, it can stay there."

"You can put a pair of marigolds on, can't you?"

"Hardy, it is not in the pan, I assure you – it's between here and the door. In fact I can see it from here."

"Is there a W and a C there as well?" he asked, seeking to prolong the toilet fun.

"No, they have gone round the U bend."

They were both aware that that had not worked quite as well, but even so was approaching fun in Hardy's mind.

Hardy had a good one, 'ferry' and on a double score.

"Very good." she admitted, staring at the word.

"Strange," she continued, "how words provoke memories." She paused. "You put that down on purpose, didn't you? I tell you now, Hardy, that day was one of the worst of my life. And to be quite frank, it was that day and your behaviour that made up my mind that we were finished."

"It seemed to me that you'd made up your mind long before then."

"I had thought things over, but when you came back from Bert's place pissed, that was really the final straw."

"I only drink because you make me miserable, you know." he retorted.

She just looked at him, not fully taking in what he had just said, and in turn not believing it. The conversation died, neither Hardy nor Joyce having the will to continue.

The game continued, but dragged a bit. It resulted in the opening of a bottle of wine. Indeed, most events resulted in a bottle of wine being opened, and it seemed like three quarters of the UK joined them. The bottle banks were always overflowing when Hardy ventured there to empty the box.

The enforcement of 'being together' yet still apart led to strange conversations.

"You've always drawled when you speak, haven't you?"

Joyce said to Hardy one afternoon, before the inevitable tedium of afternoon television.

Was this leading to another attack? Hardy prepared himself.

"I'm not aware of it, although several people have told me during my lifetime, but interestingly, never you, until now."

"Early on I found it quite endearing, but of course over time endearing traits become irritating, especially if you have fallen out of love with the individual."

She could never resist an opportunity to reinforce the rejection, even though he thought they seemed to be getting on OK at the moment.

"Where I come from in Norfolk, most people speak like me."

"Of course they do, but it takes so bloody long for you to tell a tale that people get fed up with it and move on before you have finished."

"Is that right? Well I am sorry."

"It's not a criticism, merely an observation. I remember years and years ago before I met you, there used to be this programme on Radio Two called the John Dunn show. I used to listen to it on the car radio coming home from work, and every day he used to have a little slot called 'answers please'. On this particular day he was talking about why people speaking other languages speak faster, or appear to speak faster than we do. Well they must all speak faster than you, Hardy, anyway."

"There's no need to keep digging at me, you've made your point."

"Not really and stop being such a snowflake all the time. Anyway, getting back to what I was going to say, apparently they need to speak fast in order to deliver the same message in the same time as their opponents. Like during the war, because so many German words are long, they would have to have spoken faster to deliver the same message that a different language like English could deliver in a shorter way."

"What?"

"Well, take for example, we would say, 'I am sick to death of this' - simple, but in German it is 'das alles hängt mir gründlich zum Halse raus, ich bin das alles gründlich satt' or 'leid'. So you have to say it quicker to deliver the same message.

Hardy was impressed. He could neither fault her or correct her. It was curious how this enforced 'isolation' was actually encouraging conversation, conversation about all sorts of rubbish.

"I never knew you could speak a bit of German."

"Hardy, you know very little about me. Who do you think it was that had to constantly ring the Ford plant in Niehl to get you half shafts for Cortina's?"

Indeed, he did remember her having to order stuff from them, but he'd always assumed she had spoken to someone who spoke English.

"Oh, so did you get to practise with them?"

"Hardy, you would be surprised what happened. Some of the men used to chat me up in a mixture of English and German. I soon got to know some words that a nice lady like me should not know."

"Really?"

"And do you remember, we used to get stuff quite quick, and do you know why that was? It was because that guy called Pieter used to come over to speak to the Ford people over here, and bring a couple halfshafts with him on the plane."

"You're joking! So you only got half a shaft?" Hardy thought that was both quick and funny.

Joyce knew full well what the 'joke' was, but decided that it was beneath contempt and required a retort that would hurt.

Despite the really interesting conversations, bedtime was getting earlier and earlier. Joyce read a chapter of her book before she eventually turned over and closed her eyes in an effort to shut the day down and prepare for another one, whatever the next one would bring.

Like always, the night was disturbed: waking at three o'clock seemed now the norm. Getting back to sleep was always a problem, but her dreams when she did nod off were vivid and so real – frighteningly so.

The one she worried about most was the one involving Hardy.

They were both on the Gosport ferry, outbound to Portsmouth. They had gone to the stern, where the seats were on a semi-open deck, but Hardy liked to walk around a little, looking at the scenery. Hardy always commented on Harbour Tower and Seaward Tower - the flats that overlooked the harbour. And, true to form, he said again to Joyce that he often fancied living in one of them.

The ferry sometimes revved its engines to indicate to the ticket collector that it was time to get back on board because the ferry was about to depart. The revving meant that people halfway down the pontoon started running like the wind to try and catch the ferry: it never waited for stragglers. Hardy always got some sense of satisfaction that he was 'aboard' when he could see others hurrying to catch it. In Joyce's dream, he was particularly offensive. He laughed out loud, really roaring when he saw an old lady trying desperately to reach the ferry before they closed the glass doors.

"You despicable bastard," Joyce called him.

Hardy just grinned, but the crewman let the old lady on board, which seemed to disappoint him. The 'old lady' – now looking very fit – marched towards Hardy. She was wearing an expensive pair of bright red trainers. They were absurdly big, almost like clown's shoes.

She sat down next to Joyce and gestured at Hardy leaning against the guard-rails.

"Does that piece of crap belong to you?" she asked Joyce.

The old lady's hair was white, fluffy and blowing in the wind. She wore a brown coat, close to the colour that Joyce was wearing. Joyce tried to answer, but nothing would come. As much as she tried to shout to the old lady, nothing would come out.

Two other women came over to the old lady. They were younger – one of them could be no more than twenty and the other one was probably her mother.

The ferry had left the pontoon, but was holding back for a liner that was going out of the harbour. The liner was huge, the biggest Joyce had ever seen. Hardy moved to the other side of the boat to observe it, as did the two women. The younger one had shorts on, the sort of shorts that makes the shape of the backside totally available to public gaze. Of course, Hardy stared at her rear end – it was only natural.

"What you staring at, you filthy perv?"

"He is, ain't he?" said the mother-figure.

"He's not with anyone," said the old lady. "Bloke on his own, they're always the same, think they can do what they like with us."

"Well we ain't having it," said the young girl.

Hardy was looking amused now; he had that sick grin that he sometimes wore when he knew he was in the right, when he knew he had the upper hand. Joyce despised that grin because it was mainly at her expense.

The huge liner seemed to take an age to pass, as the three women surrounded Hardy.

"We hate pervs like you," said the old lady

"Don't know what you're worried about, you old bag," said Hardy. "No chance of any lusting coming your way." He seemed proud of that.

Joyce was trying to shout to him to shut up, but nothing that was coming out of her mouth was making sense; they were just muffled noises.

The liner was leaving a huge wake; the whole harbour seemed to be foaming. There was foam blowing over to Harbour Tower, completely covering the structure, and people on the esplanade were taking cover. It was into this foaming mass that the three women decided that 'pervs' like Hardy should be done away with. As if co-ordinated, two of them grabbed one leg each, toppled him over, and then with what seemed enormous strength, because Hardy was far from light, lifted him into the air. He still had that stupid grin on his face. They held him high, and said to the old lady:

"What you want us to do with the bastard?"

"Throw him over!" shouted the old woman. With that the old woman gave Hardy a shove. He went backwards, and over the stern of the ferry.

"Oh my God!" Joyce tried to scream. "What have you done?" she tried to ask, but no words would come. She wanted to stand up and look over the side for him, but she couldn't stand for some reason, and the women had gone. The huge liner was gone, the sea was now calm, and life looked ordinary.

But where was Hardy?

Joyce woke with a start, bathed in sweat. It took her a minute or two to realise that she had dreamt about Hardy being murdered. She felt shocked and distressed: it would be good to talk about it … but there was no one to talk to.

CHAPTER SEVENTEEN
A Mystery Letter

The tea was welcome, as was the company.

"Are you going to give that watch to Mrs Burgess?" Hardy enquired.

"You want me to, don't you?"

"It just seems so crass when we've inherited a house and all she wants is a watch."

"I do know roughly what it's worth," said Joyce. "I've looked it up on the internet."

"So what is it worth?"

"About five thousand pounds."

"You're joking." Hardy was flabbergasted.

Joyce went picked up her iPad, and quickly found the page that she had saved as a 'favourite'. Indeed, there it was. Hardy crossed-checked it to the watch: Joyce was right. That presented even more of a dilemma.

"The sale of that watch would give us the capital to do something with the house."

"Not at the moment, it wouldn't. There's no shops open selling any building or decorating stuff, and I don't know whether the building trade is even working at the moment."

"They must be, I mean, how they going to live?"

"The same way as everyone else who can't go to work, I guess."

"This is ridiculous." said Joyce. She was obviously just

beginning to grasp the depth of the situation and the seriousness with which the government was taking it.

"How long you reckon this will go on for?"

"I've got no idea, and I don't think anyone else has."

Both Hardy and Joyce were slowly coming round to the idea that this crisis was beyond their control: it was beyond everyone's control, and worse of all, there was no 'playbook' for any Government in the world to follow.

"But that still doesn't answer the question as to what we are going to do with the watch," said Hardy. "I see where you are coming from, but it just makes me feel so mean and deceitful."

Joyce was taken aback by this.

"That's unlike you," she eventually said.

"What you mean, that's unlike me?"

"Normally you are up for grabbing every penny from a situation."

"Yeah, but this is different, isn't it? Mrs Burgess was a good friend to Bert and she has been really good to us as well."

Joyce was quiet and thoughtful.

"I suppose you're right, Hardy. I am being a bit selfish, aren't I?"

Hardy was overcome. Did she have the virus? Was this a symptom – suddenly becoming reasonable?

"We could tell her quite honestly that you took it home to value it, and to be sure it was safe. Then we can wrap it and make a presentation about it."

Joyce agreed this was the best course of action. Hardy was astounded to have encountered no argument.

The landline rang. As they were both downstairs and in Joyce's 'domain', she would be the one to pick it up.

"Hello."

The voice at the other end was female. It must be for him, Hardy thought.

"Yes, it is," said Joyce.

Hardy could not hear the voice properly, and now was running out of guesses as to who it was.

"Could you hold on just a second?" Joyce put her hand over the receiver, and looked towards Hardy. "It's Freya somebody, who has just flown back from Singapore. Said she wanted to chat about her uncle Bert's house."

Hardy felt his heart sink. Why on earth was she wanting to talk about something that she could change now? True to form – when he had something good, something came along and screwed it up. Reluctantly, Hardy took the phone. He could now actually feel his heart thumping with fear as to what Freya was going to say.

"Hello," he said.

"Hello, Hardy. I hope you don't mind me using your first name, but the solicitor at the town hall referred to you in that manner."

"You've been talking to him, have you?" Hardy was coming over as aggressive, more out of fear than anything else.

"Yes, he kindly gave me your phone number, and all I wanted to do is to visit Uncle Bert's house – along with you of course – to see if there are any old family photographs there."

The relief was palpable. The stress dissolved. This was perfectly reasonable thought Hardy.

"Yes, of course you can, but we are not allowed to at the moment, are we?"

"I realise that, but the reason for ringing now was to avoid the possibility of you throwing out any photographs you may come across."

"We haven't come across any yet, but then we haven't done that much round there. We've taken some clothes to the charity shop – the Salvation Army shop as it happens, as we thought you would like that. But even they are shut now."

"How thoughtful – that's really good of you. We've been flown home by the Army because of this epidemic. Things are bad in Malaysia."

"So where are you staying?"

"They are putting us up in a Salvation Army hostel in London. Not ideal, but at least we can help out with all their homeless customers. Of course, Covid has made the work so much more difficult."

"I imagine the homeless must be very vulnerable to infection."

"Yes, indeed, and yet they are out in the open all the time, and apparently the virus is harder to catch in the open air, so you'd think they would be healthier, wouldn't you?"

"I never thought of that. Well, look, as soon as you are able to leave your hostel you are welcome to come and visit us, and we will take you round the house."

Joyce was hovering like a busy bee in the background, dying to find out what Hardy had agreed to. He could have tormented her, but for reasons that he did not quite understand himself, he did not. He explained to her straight away what Freya wanted.

"That's fair enough – can't deny the girl that." Joyce said.

"Of course not, but God knows when we'll be able to do it legally."

"Well no one would question what we were doing anyway, even if we did it in the next few days."

"I doubt whether a woman like that would break rules in these circumstances. Anyway, what are you bothered about? She only wants photographs – we can easily box them up for when she can pick them up."

"We're allowed out for exercise, so we could walk round there and see what we can find for her."

"Where do you start to look for photographs in a house like this?" asked Hardy, not really expecting a reply, but he got one anyway.

"Well, where do we keep our photographs?" said Joyce. "They are in a box in what was the spare bedroom, so that's where we start here. We haven't looked in that small third bedroom much at all, have we?"

As they opened the door onto yet another darkened room, with closed curtains laden with dust, a scene greeted them that they had previously just closed the door on. There were boxes everywhere. There were paintings stacked in the corner, and a huge picture of the Gosport crest on the wall.

"Crikey, do you reckon there's a bed under this lot?"

"I hope so – if not, there are so many boxes here it will take us a month of Sundays to clear." Hardy was trying to make his way around the pile of boxes to get to the window to allow some light in, but it was proving difficult, as there was only limited space to place his size tens.

"For God's sake be careful, Hardy. I don't want to have to get an ambulance crew in here, especially while they are so busy."

"That's a relief. For one moment there I was thinking you might actually be concerned about *my* safety."

He got eventually to the window, grasped the centre of both curtains and pulled them back. Light flooded in, revealing Hardy's mackintosh now covered in fluff.

"There's fluff on your stubble too," said Joyce. "I know that's not designer stubble, it's just bits that you've missed with that old razor of yours."

There was no way she could remain without malice for more than a few minutes, thought Hardy.

Suddenly he said, "Shoe boxes."

"What?"

"Shoe boxes, that's where they will be, that's where we used to put photographs, in shoe boxes."

There were indeed shoe boxes among the pile, which included large boxes that once contained Smith's crisps (proud that they contained the salt that went into a little twisted blue bag with them), Tizer and even Player's Navy Cut cigarettes. Right on top were some documents held together by a decaying elastic band.

"I might as well start with these on the floor, to clear a bit of space," said Hardy.

"Good idea. I'll start from this end so that we make the place a bit safer."

"Are they still collecting the recycling bins?"

"I never thought of that. Let me go down to the kitchen as see if there are any bin bags. I am a twerp actually, I should have thought of this and brought some with us."

Joyce departed for the kitchen, leaving Hardy somewhat bewildered. The pair of them were actually functioning as a pair again. They had not bickered for several hours.

He heard a crash from the kitchen.

"You OK, Joyce?" he shouted.

"Yeah, load of saucepans fell out when I opened the door under the sink. Oh God, Hardy, this is disgusting, some of this hasn't been washed up, it's gone mouldy."

"We'll just have to throw them out then."

Joyce eventually spotted some garden waste bags in the lean-to and took them up to Hardy to start filling.

"We can take them up the tip," she said.

"They've closed it."

"Why?"

"Because of Covid."

"That's ridiculous, how are people going to dispose of stuff like this?"

"In farmers' fields probably." Hardy's answer, whilst frivolous, had a ring of truth to it.

Hardy was looking in a Clarks shoe box. He had found some photos in there but they made no sense to him. It was a picture of a woman on stage; it looked like she was singing but one of those big round black microphones blotted out most of her face. Hardy turned the picture over. There was writing on the back: 'many and sincere thanks from Nat G'. It meant nothing to Hardy. There were lots more pictures of a dance orchestra, some of which also featured this young woman and which looked like they were taken in the 1950s. Hardy wondered if this was Bert's mother. He was struck by how smart the band was, all in evening dress, and how slim the ladies were.

Joyce had started on a box that once housed packets of Tide washing powder.

"Do you know, Hardy, I can still smell that washing powder on this box. Reminds me of when I was a child, and the smell in shops back then."

"Yeah, I always remember the small shop at the end of the road. Mum used to send me up there with a shopping list, and it always smelt of coffee at one end and Harpic at the other end."

There were items wrapped in newspaper in the box. The top one was wrapped in a page from the *Portsmouth*

Evening News of 1962. It completely distracted her from the matter in hand.

"Hardy, look at this. This guy from the council is responding to complaints from women whose stiletto heels get stuck in the gaps between the planks on the ferry pontoon. He asked if they do not realise that the gaps open and shut with the temperature and even the ferry has no control over that. Weird, eh? We just take it for granted now that we can wear what we like to get on the ferry. In fact I had heels on the other day."

"Look at these." Hardy held up a set of photographs in an album. They were pictures of what looked like an old Portsmouth FC team.

Joyce found a pile of letters in one box; she read the first, trying to decipher the handwriting.

"'Dear Mother' it says and this is dated 1936!" she told Hardy.

"Read it out, then."

'*Dear Mother, I have been drafted to HMS Nelson, and my official title is boy telegraphist. Last Monday we went into dry dock in Pompey, but because there are about twenty of us boys on here, the ones at the top reckon the accommodation is unsuitable. You would never guess – we have to fall in on the jetty and are ferried over to your side in Gosport. We have to march through the town shouldering .303 rifles, and march all the way out to the fort they call number two battery down at Stokes Bay.*

We've been issued straw mattresses to sleep on, and we are allowed to swim, and we can go out until eight o'clock.

I have met a girl who I see most evenings. She is very pretty and lives in the village of Alverstoke. I will write again before we sail, but mother you could come over one

Sunday, after church when we are free, and we could take tea at the tea rooms.'

"And it's signed Duncan ... I wonder who he is?"

"Well, if it's 1936 he is probably dead by now, because he was probably fourteen or fifteen back then. Then he had the war to contend with – let's hope he survived it. It could be, of course, that this is Bert's dad. The dates would fit if he knocked this girl up around then or just before the war."

"Don't be so crude, I hate that term," complained Joyce.

"What term?"

"Knocked up. It's distasteful."

"Why?"

"Because it goes back to slavery days. If a young girl was thought good enough for breeding, the price was 'knocked up.' They attracted a bonus for the trader."

"Where on earth did you get that from?"

"Oh, what's that programme. It's on in the afternoons. What's it called, yes, Countdown."

This was going to take all day; they were making little progress. They had at least found some photographs for Freya, but neither Joyce or Hardy felt motivated to carry on.

Hardy woke as if it was early morning. He seemed full of energy. He turned and looked at the clock. He sighed. "Bloody five past three again." It was jet black outside, totally silent apart from the odd wisp of wind kicking the overturned watering can further from its home under the water butts. He made an abortive attempt to go back to sleep, but his mind was far too active.

"While I'm awake, I could go for a wee I suppose," he said to himself. This same routine happened nearly every night. He got out of bed too quickly again, the room was not quite stable, and he was pretty sure it was not down to an earthquake. The usual thing happened; he only just made it to the toilet, and the fluorescent light took longer than normal to break into action, so for the first five seconds he could not see quite where he was aiming. The floorcloth would be required again, he thought. He mopped the floor with his foot using the cloth; he was not going to risk getting down on hands and knees. He got himself some water and made it back to his bed without stubbing his toe on the chair. His calf muscles started to hurt and he wondered whether it was cramp or something more serious. He had time to concentrate on it, there, alone in the dark. He had a habit of scratching, especially when he was nervous, and so now he started scratching his arm.

The events of the day started to replay in his mind, the pictures they had found, the teapot in the box, the silver cutlery, and the dead mouse, a mouse that must have believed food was readily available on that bed but that, had alas, died of starvation.

'Or perhaps of old age,' thought Hardy.

Just like other nights, his mind turned to his own age, and the fact that every day that passed was now quite noticeable and that his bucket of sand was running out. He lay there in the dark, wondering how he was going to die. Would it be a quick heart attack, or would he have an illness, as yet undiagnosed, but quietly working away at his body already? He could drive himself into depression quite easily, and develop symptoms relating to all sorts of conditions. But for now, he was aware of his deep vein thrombosis. He felt his calf, yes it was hot and hard.

He decided he could do nothing about it now, and should return to the ambition of sleep. He turned onto his right side, which would, in the old days, have been turning away from Joyce. That was the side on which he always went to sleep, and by adopting the same position as earlier in the night, he reasoned that he should be able to nod off again.

He turned again. He remembered turning in the past to find Joyce, usually quietly snoring. He would cuddle her and she would respond in her sleep. He reasoned again that this situation was so false, that Joyce really didn't understand what she was doing. Look at today, they hadn't argued at all, in fact they had been on the brink of having a laugh. Why couldn't she be like that all the time?

He turned over again, but this time felt a pain in the side of his back. Nothing unusual there – just cramp, he told himself. On the other hand, it could be something more serious. He worried that it was his liver. He was a prime candidate for that: he knew his drinking had got worse without Joyce to control it.

"Wonder what the time is?" He looked at the clock again. Still only half-past three.

Joyce had been awakened by the movement upstairs. Cursing, she got up to use the loo. Might just as well, now I'm awake, she reasoned.

"Bloody man, even though he's upstairs, he still has the ability to wake me up."

As she sat on the loo, she noticed a large spider heading towards her. Why did it have to do that now, at this point, and in the middle of the bloody night? She was not scared of spiders in normal circumstances, but this one seemed to be on a mission. It seemed, although she was sure she was seeing things, that it had more legs than other spiders. Her PJ bottoms were now only about twelve inches from being invaded. If that happened, she might well have to scream, she thought. She thought quickly, screwed up some toilet paper and threw it at the spider. Bang on target! The spider suspended its march towards her.

She pulled up her PJs, relieved that no knight in shining armour had had to be summoned from upstairs, and set about finding a jam jar and a piece of card, so she could put the spider out of the back door. There was a jar at the back of the cups. Everything seemed to be at the back of something else these days, because of lack of space. And it was this lack of space that led to the crash. Her elbow knocked over onto the floor a stack of cups.

"Bugger!" she exclaimed, knowing what would happen next. And sure enough, it did.

"Joyce! Joyce, you alright?" Hardy was already making his way down the stairs.

"Yes, Hardy, thank you! Just knocked these cups over."

"What on earth are you up to?"

The question irritated Joyce beyond belief. Through gritted teeth she said:

"I am trying to get an empty jam jar."

This only threw marginal light into Hardy's confused mind.

"There is a spider in the toilet, and I am looking for a jam jar and a bit of card or something so I can put him outside."

"Well, be careful how you get up or you'll cut your feet on that broken stuff. Here, let me get the dustpan."

Hardy leapt across the room, immediately cutting his foot on a piece of cup that had obviously taken off in its own trajectory, and had landed a good yard away.

"Fuck!"

"Oh for God's sake. Look, you are getting blood all over

the floor."

"Oh great – is that all you are worried about?"

He got a dishcloth off of the sink draining board and pressed it to his foot.

"Can you get me my slippers? We don't want both of us in the same state as you," said Joyce, "but try not to bleed on the bedroom carpet."

Hardy limped into her bedroom, the room that had previously been their lounge and got her slippers. Of course, he got blood on the carpet. How could he not, he reasoned to himself? His foot was now hurting.

"Right, sit down. Let's look at this foot of yours," she said. Hardy took one of the kitchen stools, while Joyce attended to the wound. "This is not pleasant. When did you last cut your toenails?"

"Well, I heard years ago that one way a woman can check if a guy is single or not, is whether he cuts his toenails."

"What?"

"Wives ensure that they are not scarred in the night by their husband's sharp and rough nails. If they have long toenails, it means they've got no wife to nag them into cutting them shorter."

"Never heard that before, and for a long time you didn't file your nails down," she countered.

She put some TCP on the wound, which sent Hardy into orbit. She got a mild sense of power and enjoyment from that.

"Peculiar how the smell of TCP is almost comforting," Hardy said.

"I guess it reminds people of hospital."

Hardy tentatively put his foot on the floor, it was going to hurt, and the tea-towel bandage Joyce had put on meant he was a bit lopsided.

"This is ridiculous isn't it?" Joyce eventually said. "Quarter to four in the morning, you with a cut foot, a pile of broken cups on the floor, both of us in PJs and a spider in the toilet probably scared to death of what's going on. If they made a TV programme of it, everyone would think it was exaggerated."

They both chuckled, able to see the funny side of the predicament they were in.

"I won't be able to get back to sleep now – do you want a cup of tea?" Joyce asked.

"Only if you can find a cup to put it in."

"Ha-ha, very funny. Most of that stuff on the floor is stuff we haven't used in years. It came from your mother if you remember, she had a complete set."

Hardy didn't remember: he remembered little of what had gone on when his mother had died. Joyce had taken care of pretty much everything, even telling Hardy what to say at the funeral. He had been busy with the business at the time, and in any case he had not been particularly fond of his mother. She was dominant, always making him feel guilty about something or other. Ever since his father had died, she had made him responsible for her, but Joyce saw to that once he had married her. It wasn't for a number of years that Hardy realised that he had merely replaced one dominant and controlling female with another.

CHAPTER EIGHTEEN
A Meeting with Freya

The initial lockdown was lifting in small steps, and a phone call from Freya struck both excitement and trepidation that at last they were to meet their generous benefactor.

"Wonder what she will be like?" pondered Hardy

"Pretty pointless question, isn't it? You are going to meet her in two hours. Are you meeting her at the ferry?"

"Yeah, but I think I'll drive down and pick her up, you can meet us round at the house."

"I'll let you two get there first. I've got to the point where I cannot stand the place; it really does give me the heebie jeebies."

"I'd rather you went there first. It might not be a good idea for me to take a young lady into an empty house, she might feel uncomfortable."

With all the publicity around 'wicked' men at the moment, even Joyce had to concede that Hardy might well have a point.

Hardy was relieved that the issue of the watch was now resolved, and apparently without falling out with Mrs Burgess. Joyce had told Mrs Burgess that she had found the watch before she knew that Mrs Burgess wanted it, and had had it valued. Mrs Burgess had accepted that explanation, although Hardy was aware that 'female looks' had been exchanged between her and Joyce. He was aware that these silent signals were not something that men could interpret. Mrs Burgess knew, and had let Joyce know she knew, but no verbal exchange had happened. So life could go on.

Hardy finished his cereal. His tea was next, along with his multi-vitamin pill. Over the past few weeks, Joyce had reverted to her old role of providing breakfast. But – and she would be first to point this out – it was different from a year ago because they were actually having a conversation over breakfast. Although the subject matter was pretty much always the same, at least they were talking. The subject, of course, was the house and the uphill struggle in sorting it out.

They had piled up stuff that might be of interest to Freya. She had started taking an interest in her 'roots' and wondered whether there might be photographs of her mother and father who were now both 'promoted to glory', as they said in the Salvation Army.

"I rather like that," Hardy had said to Joyce after the telephone conversation. "Promoted to glory – gives a sense of improvement after death."

"Wouldn't it be great if we actually knew?"

"Knew what?"

"What happens when we die."

"I thought you believed in the teachings of the church? If you have been a good girl you will get everlasting life, and if you have been a bad one you go off to the devil to an eternal fire."

"Yes, but there's no proof, is there?"

"But what choice have you got? You either believe it, or you don't. I suppose in years gone by it was a way of keeping the population in order. If God said it was wrong, it was wrong, and if you went against it you would have this terrible sentence hanging over you. Hey, but wait, you can renew your membership of the good club with just one visit to a box with a priest."

"Oh, stop it, Hardy, that's Catholic anyway."

"But the whole idea of all Christian religion is that no matter what bad you have done, there is a way back, provided you ask for forgiveness."

"It's not as frivolous as that, and in any case, you have been with me in church for the past God knows, how many years, so you know as much as I do ... if you were paying attention."

He ignored the last bit.

The green-and-white ferry left the Portsmouth side, as it had done for centuries. But things were different now because they were only running one ferry every quarter of an hour, and even then they were nearly empty. Many of the regulars who used it to commute to work were working from home or had been furloughed. Portsmouth Naval base was not working at anywhere near capacity, and hence even in the morning, passenger numbers were well down. People were not going to the Gunwharf shopping and leisure centre, with cinemas closed as well as bowling alleys and restaurants. Hardly a shop in the centre qualified as essential, so the place was deserted apart from the residents of the luxury flats. Hardy envied those: harbour views, restaurants, cinemas, shops and railway station all on their doorstep. But now all was dead, silent and without life.

Freya was not easy to spot as she emerged from the pontoon, but then again there was only a few people actually using the ferry. She must be the tall and slim young woman, dressed in jeans and short coat, but she did not look like a Salvation Army Officer. But then she was the only woman coming out of the pontoon tunnel. He could not see her face yet; she wore a mask as all passengers were obliged to do, but she had a definite femininity about her.

She spotted Hardy, which was not difficult in the deserted pick-up area, and he spotted her, and in one of those curious actions that strangers are capable of, they both seemed to know that it was the other one they were there to meet. In a funny way, it reminded Hardy of his skirmishes with the online dating scene. He immediately told himself not to be so silly, this was not a date, although, looking at her, he was wishing it was.

He raised his arm to wave, and in the twenty or so paces she took to reach him, she removed her face mask. Hardy was not disappointed. She had golden blonde hair, cut fairly short but not in a masculine way. She wore makeup, which he had not expected. Her shoes had heels, and indicated to Hardy some sophistication. She carried what appeared to be an overnight bag.

"Hello, Hardy," she said. Again, she exuded sophistication. He could detect no accent – it was almost what used to be regarded as BBC English before they went on their 'inclusive' drive.

"Hello, Freya. I've brought the car down – it's just over there. The house isn't far, but I thought the last thing you would need now is a twenty-minute walk."

"Thank you. It's very good of you."

"Not at all, it's the least we can do."

Hardy turned to lead the way to the car, to be greeted by Ken. Why on earth was he here? Was he haunting them, turning up at difficult moments?

"Hi, Hardy."

"Oh, hello Ken."

Ken eyed the lovely Freya then looked at Hardy in a 'wink wink nod nod' manner, which Hardy found embarrassing.

"This is Freya, she's Bert's niece."

"Not another of your dates then," said Ken, thinking that was riotously funny.

"She is here to go through some of Bert's stuff, which we have sorted out for her. Freya, this is a friend of mine – Ken."

"Pleased to meet you," said Ken. "Your uncle Bert was a good friend of mine – in fact I was with him on the day he died, as was Hardy here."

"You were both with him?"

"Yes, we were on a demo with him, a protest," Ken informed her.

Hardy was far from happy with this line of conversation but failed to change the subject.

"A demo?" she asked.

"I'll tell you all about it during today," Hardy interrupted. "We can't hang around, Ken – we have a lot to do."

"Of course you do, mate. See you later."

And with that they started to walk away towards the car.

"So you are meeting him later today?" Freya asked.

Hardy was bemused at first, but then realised.

"I see what you mean, no, it's just something we say. 'Later' can mean next year, or even just the next time they see you."

"I'd just not heard that before."

They approached the car and he clicked the remote control, unlocking the doors about three yards before they reached it. As he drove her to the house, he found he was sweating with nerves, whereas she seemed completely relaxed. He felt the need to speak.

"My wife is meeting us at the house, and she has made us all a sandwich for lunch. But it would be better if you ate that round at our house."

"That's very kind of you."

"It's not a problem, I mean, where would you eat anyway? Everything is shut."

"That's true."

"I hope this doesn't appear rude, but can I ask what time train you're getting back?'

"Oh, I thought I'd stay overnight in the house, if you don't mind, and travel back tomorrow around midday, so I'm back in London before dark."

Hardy was gobsmacked. Overnight? Had the woman no idea of the state of the place? Hardy had assumed that the bag she carried was to accommodate any 'spoils' she might take from the house, but alas no, it must accommodate her overnight kit.

"You may change your mind when you see the state of the place. There has been no heating in it for ages, and none of the beds are aired. They're probably damp, and goodness knows what's in them. There may be all sorts of things in those beds to share the night with you."

"I guess I need to see it first, don't I? I can tell you, Hardy, that I've slept in some pretty unpleasant places during my career with the Army."

"Have you? How does that happen?"

"I've done missionary work with them. I mean, I didn't have to sleep in tribal huts or anything, just in accommodation that – shall we say – needed some loving."

Hardy had failed to appreciate that the Salvation Army were still an 'outreach' organisation, and there was nowhere in the world that they would not go. Freya was not what he had expected: she was very attractive woman, but also one wise to the world.

He also thought that her attitude was a bit presumptive. He could actually be living in the house and she had effectively invited herself to stay the night.

"Hardy, I'm winding you up. You should have seen your face when I said I was staying. Of course I'm not, it's not my house to stay in."

Hardy was relieved and mildly amused that she was taking the mickey.

She continued: "No, I'm getting the five-fifty back to Waterloo this afternoon, and the bag is to hold anything you may allow me to take."

"Did you know Bert's parents?" Hardy eventually asked.

"Yes, I went to his mother's funeral. She was a lady of elegance as I remember, very dignified, but then I was very young."

"We rather gathered that from the clothes in her wardrobe."

"She's been dead for years, but her clothes are still there?"

"Yes, dresses, coats, all manner of things. We've not been able to dispose of it, because all the secondhand shops are shut. My wife says it's all very good quality, and far too good to just throw out. Although I doubt whether anyone would wear the stuff these days."

"That doesn't surprise me. There are so few events where dress is an important factor nowadays," she said.

They arrived at the house and Hardy searched for a space to park.

"Is that one over there?" said Freya.

"It's a bit small," said Hardy, noting that the spot was

only just longer than the car.

"You can get this in there."

It seemed like a challenge: he had to do it now. He crunched into reverse and steered hard to the right just behind the parked car in front. He then mounted the pavement with his rear wheel.

"Bugger!" he said, then "sorry – I didn't mean to swear."

"It's no problem, we all say things in these circumstances. I'm fine with that, I just don't like the Lord's name taken in vain."

"Yeah, I get that," he said as he pulled out into the road again. He figured he needed to straighten up just that little bit earlier. By now he was panicking. His efforts to impress this lovely lady were failing. The engine was revving unnecessarily, something that years ago he had noticed 'older' people doing. He swore he would never do that, now here he was demonstrating the art of slipping the clutch at high revs. He attempted the manoeuvre again, this time straightening up much earlier: he was in the spot, and as far as Hardy was concerned, that was good enough.

Freya looked at him, almost pityingly. He turned the engine off and struggled out of the car. It was only at this point that he could see the car was about two feet out into the road, and Freya was having to take a huge leap to get to the kerb. Hardy decided that he could live with this: he was not moving it again.

"Lots of roads are like this in Gosport," he said, weakly. She didn't respond, but was pointing to the house.

"That's it, isn't it? That's the house over there. I can't think how long ago it was when I was last here."

Hardy was now intent on getting inside. They hadn't even changed the locks from the reliable old Yale that presented itself halfway up the dark brown front door. Mrs

Burgess next door had invested in a new composite door, with internal lock levers all over the place, and it did make a real difference to the presentation of the house. The door cracked open, and the now familiar smell greeted Hardy. However, this time it was mixed with the aroma of Joyce's perfume, a blessed relief. Hardy had not expected her to be in the house in view of her previous comments. She was here, however, and the thought of this lovely young lady being in this house with him on their own faded to a stupid fantasy.

"Joyce!" he shouted as the entered the front door.

"Hi," Joyce returned, so pleasantly that it took Hardy back a bit. She emerged from the kitchen along the rather dark passageway by the stairs.

"This is my wife Joyce. Joyce, this is Freya."

"Hello Freya, nice to meet you at long last, Freya. Did you have a good journey, Freya?"

Hardy had witnessed this repeating of a name lots of times in the past. Joyce had read how Margaret Thatcher remembered people's names by repeating the name quickly in the first one or two opening sentences in any conversation. Joyce was employing that method now, and not hiding it very well because it came over as absurd.

Freya wrinkled her nose.

"Yes, sorry, we have not been able to get rid of the smell yet, even though we have ditched all the stale food in the kitchen, and put some disinfectant down the toilets to freshen them up a bit."

Freya held out a hand to greet Joyce, then remembered:

"Oh, we're not meant to do that any more, are we?"

"No, I don't think so. Do you want a cup of tea?" Joyce asked. "Don't worry," she said, seeing Freya's doubtful expression. "I've brought round several mugs from home. There are fresh tea bags here and fresh milk."

"Well in that case, yes please."

Freya followed the pair into the kitchen, observing all the time.

"I remember this kitchen, it always had a smell of gas in the air."

There were envelopes carefully laid out on the table, the table that Bert and Hardy had sat at that last afternoon. Hardy covered the stain where the brandy had stripped the polish. He did it unconsciously; it troubled him because it reminded him of his guilt in Bert's death. Mrs Burgess had tried to blank out the stain, but had singularly failed.

"Have you ever met Mrs Burgess next door?" asked Hardy. "She was the lady who found Bert."

"I may have done, but it was so long ago, and I probably wouldn't recognise her now."

There was a slight bang as Joyce lit the gas under the kettle.

"Cripes, this is really going back in time," Freya said.

"It could become a nice house, though," said Hardy. "I've seen what Mrs Burgess has done next door. Anyway, I have put all the photos we have found up to the moment in envelopes here on the table. We have not thrown any out, but because there were so many of them, I have put ones that don't include people into that big envelope over there."

Freya pulled out a chair to sit down. It was the very chair on which Bert had died. She took some photographs out of the nearest envelope and started flipping through them.

"So what was this demo business?" she casually asked.

Joyce looked round curious as to how the subject had come up.

"We met Ken down at the ferry terminal, who told Freya that we'd been with Bert the day he died," Hardy explained to Joyce. "At the …. small protest."

"That Ken is a right stirrer."

"Look," he said to Freya, "there was no harm in it. It was just a group of pensioners that wanted the ferry – the one you have just crossed on – to be included in the bus pass scheme. You see, there are few medical facilities in Gosport and most people have to go to a hospital called QA, which is over in Portsmouth, and it can get quite expensive if you are having to go to several appointments, or visiting someone who's an in-patient there. So we organised a demonstration on the ferry. We originally were going to hijack it, but that … shall we say proved too ambitious."

"I should think it did. Was Uncle Bert on this demo with you?"

"Yes and no. He was very ill – that had become obvious to all of us – and the heat on that day was doing him in. I told him to go home."

"And that's the last you saw of him?"

"No, unfortunately we thought he had our protest banner with him, so I had to come up here to get it. Then I had a drink with him."

"Rather more than one drink!" said Joyce, still standing by the gas stove.

"Yes, OK, I had too much, I know, and to be frank, your Uncle Bert was not used to it."

"Not used to what?" Freya asked in all innocence.

That made Hardy feel even worse.

"Freya," said Joyce, "Hardy carries lots of guilt for what happened that afternoon. And to a degree, so he should."

"Really? why?"

"Go on then, Hardy." Joyce was enjoying this.

"Well … he had a bottle of brandy, and he and we practically drank the lot."

Freya just looked at him.

"I think it gave him some relief from the pain he was in," said Hardy weakly.

"Oh dear. I mean I don't know too much about the effects of alcohol from a personal point of view, I am just guessing that you both drank rather a lot. But Uncle Bert was in the final stages of cancer anyway, as I understand it. I don't think you should burden yourself with guilt in that way. He was pretty out of it when he passed away."

"So was Hardy, Freya, I can assure you, utter disgrace." Joyce loved twisting a knife.

"He was sitting where you are now." Hardy just threw that in for good measure.

"Are any of these of Bert?" asked Freya.

"I think so, but they mainly feature his parents."

"Oh yes, that's her, that's his mum."

Hardy looked over Freya's shoulder at the photograph.

"That dress is still up in the wardrobe, you know."

"I know you said he'd kept her clothes, but that dress must be more than fifty years old."

"And it's as good as new," said Joyce. "It's a ballroom dress."

"Here she is on stage with Nat Gonella – he came from Gosport, you know."

Hardy thought back to the 'NG' initials on the back of one of the photos and it all became clear.

"There's a monument to him up the road," he said. He had also compiled some press cuttings; although he could not make any connection between them and Bert, Freya might be able to cast some light on their relevance.

She homed in on one and began to read aloud:

"'Harry and Bessie Sinclair were Victorian people, but at the turn of the century became along with everyone else Edwardian. Their lives were bound up with the Gosport waterfront. Harry Sinclair had served aboard the Royal Yacht 'Osborne II' for nine years as Master at Arms. He left the service in 1894 to take up employment with the Port of Portsmouth Floating Bridge Company. Harry had been very much respected on the Royal Yacht, and had been presented with a silver-plated breakfast service.'

"What's a breakfast service?" Freya broke off her reading.

"Don't know – and why did he keep that cutting?" asked Joyce.

"Maybe the 'breakfast service' is among the boxes in that bedroom," said Hardy.

"Oh, is there more?" Freya had not seen the upstairs yet.

"I should say so. The bed – we hope there is a bed under there somewhere – in the back bedroom is covered in boxes and other forms of debris, and we haven't dared look in the loft yet," said Hardy.

Freya had returned to the photographs.

"I feel like a child in a sweet shop with all this lot."

"Probably the best thing is just to take them back home with you."

"We don't have any room to store anything. Our furniture from the UK has been in storage now for three years, and probably would have been for another three if the pandemic hadn't forced the Army to bring us both back home."

Freya turned over a larger black-and-white photograph featuring a group of people.

"That's me, that's mum and dad, hundred percent sure!"

"And I can see Bert at the back." Hardy was still leaning over her shoulder, which Joyce was finding irritating. Why couldn't he give the girl some space? Poor girl must be feeling his breath on her face. "And there's an elderly lady in the centre."

"I don't remember this at all," said Freya.

"You're probably only about three years old there, so I'm not surprised."

"I don't have many photographs of mum and dad."

"Are they … where do they live now?" asked Hardy.

"They both died relatively young."

She turned the picture over to find that someone had written names on the back – the elderly lady turned out to be Granny Sinclair, thus solving the puzzle of the newspaper cutting.

Joyce was still watching over the kettle: there was never a truer saying than 'a watched kettle never boils'. She had had enough of it, and assumed it was hot enough to make the tea.

Freya offered to go up into the loft but Joyce immediately said it was too dangerous.

"I tell you what," said Freya, "I will just stand on a chair and peer up there. It may be empty, in which case you don't ever need to go up."

"Good idea," said Hardy.

"Could you steady me, Hardy?" she asked.

He found himself with his arms around her lower waist, and within two inches of one of the nicest bums he could recall seeing.

Freya seemed totally unfazed by this and as she reached to push the loft hatch to one side, her jeans accentuated her shape even more.

"I need a torch, can't see a thing." Freya exclaimed.

"Don't move, I know where there is one. I'll get it," said Hardy

Joyce followed him, in order mainly to give him some 'advice'.

"Do you really have to hold her that tight?"

"Jealous, are you?"

"Oh come on! Do you really think a woman of her calibre would be interested in an ageing lump of lard like you?"

The torch revealed what they feared. The loft was full to the top with 'rubbish'.

"Oh, luv us, I think there is something alive over there, and there's a really peculiar smell," said Freya.

"Well, I suspect it's rotting corpses of one thing or another, they always say that where there is livestock, there's dead stock."

Freya didn't quite understand that, but decided not to pursue the issue.

"I think, if you don't mind I'll shut this hatch to this loft now, and if it were me, I would get in somebody to both clear it and fumigate it."

There was an outbreak of agreement at that suggestion.

There it was: a chalked message on a blackboard at the entrance to the Gosport Ferry.

'Trains to Waterloo are cancelled from 1600 due to lack of drivers'.

What was Hardy going to do with her? He couldn't just throw her out of the car and tell her to look after herself.

"This damned virus is really beginning to bite, isn't it?" Hardy proffered.

"So what are my options? All hotels and B&Bs are shut." she said. "I need to ring Ian, that's my husband."

She walked around with the ubiquitous mobile attached to her hand and ear. After about two minutes, she came back over to the car.

"I suppose there is no chance I could stay the night at your place? My husband will drive down and pick me up in the morning if the trains are still not running."

What could Hardy say? He felt he should help a fellow Christian.

"Let me give Joyce a ring."

Freya withdrew while Hardy made the call.

"Well, she can't stay round the house, that's out of the question," said Joyce. "All those beds will be damp. She'll have to stay round here."

"There is one problem there, though, isn't there?"

"Yes – how we explain the sleeping arrangements."

"We have to be honest with her – if she wants to stay, she'll have to put up with it."

"Put her up on the couch?" Hardy asked.

"No, of course not. I'll tell her that we are quite prepared to sleep in the double bed for one night."

Hardy was stunned into silence.

"No funny business, mind you," Joyce quickly added.

What was he meant to say to that?

"Of course not" was the only sensible response in these circumstances.

Joyce explained to Freya that she'd made up a bed downstairs because they were a bit cramped for space upstairs.

"Do you want anything to eat? I can rustle you up some bacon and egg, or there's a Cornish pasty in Hardy's bit of the fridge."

She suddenly realised sounded odd thing to say. Hardy had not heard it; he was taking his coat off in the hall. Maybe she should tell Freya the truth.

"I am a bit hungry, so that would be very nice of you indeed."

Joyce showed her the bed; of course, it was Joyce's bed. The room was suspiciously kitted out like a bedroom, quite unlike a normal day room with a put-u-up in it. And besides, this had been done too quickly.

Freya was far from an idiot but was also circumspect, and made no comment. Unless they chose to talk about anything, she was not in the business of raising issues.

After Freya had eaten, they all sat in the one room available downstairs; the telly was on to give some distraction. Hardy was aware of a tension: the elephant in the room.

"You've probably realised that the layout of this house is not quite right," said Joyce.

"I'm just grateful to have a roof over my head in these circumstances. Of course, as my husband said, in strict terms we are breaking the law. Do you have a bubble?"

"Not as such – the only person we see is Mrs Burgess, so I suppose she is the closest we get to it."

"We used to go to church every Sunday," added Hardy. It was true, but somehow it sounded false when he said it.

"All that has been cancelled and we miss it terribly," said Joyce, "which I'm sure you do too."

"Yes, of course, but being in Singapore we were seldom called upon to lead worship."

"What did you do out there, then?"

"Mainly admin, not terribly exciting. But Singapore is a great place to be, apart from the humidity and heat. It is so wealthy, yet there are pockets of extreme poverty. There is also a thriving sex and drugs industry, which we were trying to give people a way out of."

"It's a problem all over the world, isn't it?" Hardy asked.

"Pretty much. Sometimes the youngsters see dealers as role models. You can imagine, if you are living in the inner city with poor housing, poor education and little to hope for in the future, that when you see a guy driving a Bimmer, wearing gold rings and bracelets and designer clothes … he becomes an example of a way out of the grind. Often it's drugs that get them out. Maybe some get lucky and become a boxer or footballer, but they are few and far between."

"I'd never looked at it that way," Hardy said after a few seconds silence.

"But then some people, and probably me, would say hard work gets you out of anything," added Joyce.

"Yes, but you have to find work in the first place. Once you are so-called 'self-employed' you become used to having big money relatively easily. Women in particular are at risk – they get into using drugs, and then find they need to supplement their income by selling their bodies."

"It's terrible," said Joyce with a sigh. "I wonder what effect this pandemic is having on all that?"

"It makes it harder for dealers," said Freya. "With the streets deserted at night, the police can pick off dealers quite easily."

"But the sex trade must be dead. I mean how can you have sex maintaining social distancing?" Hardy seemed somewhat concerned.

"Trust you to think of that!" Joyce snapped back. She thought a change of subject was called for. "So, your husband couldn't make it today?" she asked Freya.

"No, he felt that with the restrictions, it would be better if I travelled alone, but that's rather backfired now."

"I would have thought travelling by car would have been the best option, that way you're not in contact with anyone and you could have taken back more stuff," Joyce said.

"Yeah, you could have taken that dress back," Hardy joked. They all gave a wry smile.

"I expect Ian would get quite excited seeing me wearing that!"

She was turning out to be quite a girl, thought Hardy.

"But it's so retro," said Joyce, who clearly didn't view it as a sexy bit of clothing. Early on in their marriage, Joyce had been keen to dress enticingly for Hardy, but in the past ten to fifteen years, she had stopped doing it. If Joyce appeared sexy these days, it was by accident rather than design.

"Exactly," said Freya. "It's from a different time, a different culture almost. Much more elegant than we are today, so in a bizarre sort of way it becomes rather sexy."

Joyce looked blank.

"You have to do all sorts of things to keep a marriage alive," Freya continued. "Marriage is one of the gifts God gives us; it is precious, yet all too often it is thrown onto the scrap heap without even making the minimum of effort to put things right."

There was a silence while Joyce and Hardy both wondered whether she was talking about them, and where she was going with this.

"Yes, but if married life is an absolute misery, is it worth it?" said Joyce, hitting back. "Life is so short – happiness is surely everyone's right."

"Well you two have been married for many years, I'm

guessing, and you've probably had some ups and downs, but you're still obviously still in love."

Stunned silence enveloped the room.

"Look, Freya," said Joyce after a moment, "it's best that you know what the situation is here – Hardy and I are living apart, but for financial reasons under the same roof, at the moment."

Freya's jaw dropped.

"I'm amazed to hear you say that. But how does it work with you both living here? I've never heard of this kind of arrangement."

"Basically, he lives upstairs and I live downstairs," said Joyce. Freya giggled. Both Joyce and Hardy looked at her. "What's funny?" asked Joyce.

"Well, it's a bit like a sitcom, isn't it?"

"It may be a sitcom to you, but for us it's been very painful."

"For both of you?" Freya asked, "Or is it just one sided?"

"I didn't want it to happen," said Hardy, "but we were always at one another's throats. She had no respect for me whatsoever." Hardy was looking to Joyce for confirmation.

"I wouldn't say that entirely. You let yourself down quite often, Hardy, and very often it's the drink."

"Well it's horse-and-cart, isn't it? I drink to avoid the reality of life, which in turn seems to turn you off me completely."

"Of course it does," said Joyce. "You become stupid. When you were on that date the other week with whats-her-name, she went off with that other guy, didn't she? I reckon it was because you were drinking more and more, and she could see where it was going."

"Yes, but it was *your* date that she went off with!"

"Let's get this right," said Freya, looking bewildered. "You went on a foursome?"

"Heavens, no! It's just that we both ended up in the same restaurant with our dates. Then Ken came in with his wife – you met him briefly down the ferry – and insisted we all sit together."

"Oh goodness," she said between laughing, "You couldn't make this up, could you? Maybe you weren't ready to date," she added in an effort appear more concerned than she had been in the last few minutes.

"It's certainly very difficult, dating after all these years," said Joyce. "And online seems to be the only option these days. Some of the free chat-sites are disgusting, so I chose one where I paid – that way, anyone you meet is likely to be a bit more serious about finding a relationship."

"You paid?" Hardy quickly interrupted.

"Yes, didn't you?"

"No, I bloody didn't. How much did you fork out on that?" The old financial prudence clicked in. He still regarded money as his domain.

There was a pause in the conversation until Freya said:

"I think you're both wrong about separating, but if things are as bad as you claim, Joyce,
why can't one of you move into Bert's old house?"

Joyce jumped in quickly.

"You couldn't ask anyone to move in there at the moment – it's horrible."

"So you do care a bit then, Joyce," said Freya.

"As a fellow human ... yes."

"Do you remember when you loved each other?"

"Of course," said Hardy. "It was just before the Dead Sea reported sick."

Joyce had heard that old joke numerous times, but Freya

obviously hadn't. She giggled again. She seemed be enjoying this evening.

"I remember. It was when he was young and had prospects. And for years we were very happy until the subject of children came up."

"Yes, it all went belly-up then."

"I thought it was Hardy's fault that we couldn't conceive," said Joyce, "and I did a very stupid thing. I went off with another man one night, to see if I could get pregnant. I didn't even like him that much."

"You've never said you didn't like him," piped up Hardy.

'Well it wasn't until the other day that you told me you had actually cared."

"Hey guys, hold it." Freya intervened. "Let me get this straight – Hardy, you knew that your wife had gone off with another man?"

"I assumed it – she had been dancing with this bloke and they disappeared. She didn't get back to our hotel room until the early hours of the morning, and she reeked of sex. When she came in, I just rolled over and pretended not to care, but in reality I cried myself to sleep. I only told her that a couple of weeks ago."

"That's true," Joyce confirmed. "I wanted him to have a row with me. I wanted him to show he cared because by the time I got back to the hotel I felt genuinely distressed. I never even knew the bloke's name and it went through my head that if I was pregnant by this man, then the child would never know its father … and how unfair would that be? And I would be asking Hardy to pay to bring up another man's child. I don't think I could have lived with it."

Hardy thought about this for a moment.

"I'll be honest with you, when I pretended not to care, I

wanted to hurt her and I know Joyce well enough to know that no reaction is more hurtful than anything."

Joyce had not heard that explanation before.

"You bastard," she said. "I can't believe you could have been that calculating. Just think back – if you hadn't have reacted in that way, our lives could have been very different."

"The outcome could have been that he ditched you there and then," suggested Freya.

"Do you know, in all these years it has never crossed my mind that Hardy would have done anything like that," said Joyce.

"Had you thought of ditching her, Hardy?" asked Freya.

"No, I hadn't given any thought to breaking us up. I would have had a nice two or three months of having the moral upper hand, that's all."

"I would say that you both knew that the bond you had, while ruptured by Joyce's actions, could not be broken that easily," said Freya. "Your relationship was stronger than you thought, and to my mind it still is."

CHAPTER NINETEEN
A Whispered Conversation

It was getting late by Joyce and Hardy's standards. Hardy was wondering quietly how the sleeping arrangements were going to play out. Half-past nine was often plenty late enough for Hardy, who by then was usually nodding off from the effects of alcohol. Many an evening, he didn't know what time it was or what programmes he had missed on television. Every morning when he woke up he would tell himself that this habitual drinking had to stop. However, tonight he had fought it and won. He was pleased with himself and got up, saying he was off to bed, leaving Joyce to sort out Freya.

"What do you need?" she asked. "I'll get you a towel and we have a drawer full of toothbrushes. There is some toothpaste down here in the downstairs toilet, but you will need to come upstairs for a shower if you want one in the morning."

"I know this is a bit of an imposition, but do you have a shirt or something that I could wear in bed?"

Joyce understood. This was a woman thing. While most men would climb into bed with just pants on, it wasn't an option for a woman in a stranger's house.

"Hardy!" she shouted. Hardy was halfway up the stairs, an event that seemed to take him longer and longer, especially when sober. It was always easier under the influence of alcohol.

"Have you got a clean shirt that Freya could wear overnight?"

He sorted one out and threw it down the stairs. Eventually Joyce arrived. It was now just gone ten. All in all, Joyce felt exhausted. The evening had been tiring and revealing for both of them, and she now flopped into the armchair.

"What a day!" she said.

"You can say that again. She's lovely, though."

"Yes, she is – very confident and thoughtful, yet still got both feet on the ground. Not what I was expecting at all."

They realised they would need to speak in whispers – Joyce was well aware that conversations could heard downstairs, so she got up again and closed the door. It was a signal to Hardy that, as late as it was, there was going to be an inquest into the evening's discussions.

"It was a bit like a marriage guidance session, wasn't it?" said Hardy.

"She seemed to know us so well, even though she has only just met us. I mean she's right – most of our problems have stemmed from bad communication. Anyway, are you sleeping on the settee tonight? I brought up some bedding for you."

"No, I'm bloody not – I can't sleep on this with all my aches and pains. Anyway, that's my bed in there, not yours … as you keep reminding me."

Joyce was silent for a few seconds, which when one is in the moment always seem like an eternity.

"If you were any sort of gentleman, you would willingly sleep on that settee, and allow me the comfort of a bed."

"I'm not stopping you from sleeping in the bed – it's just

that I will be in it as well."

"You crafty old git. Have you been playing this out in your mind all evening?"

Hardy was pensive: she had not hit the roof like he had expected her to do, but seemed almost pleased that he had connived to get to this situation.

"The offer is there if you want it."

"Come on then," she said. "No funny business, mind!"

"No of course not."

It took Joyce a good half hour to get into bed. She had make-up to remove, hair to brush, then there would be that catchy toenail, then her teeth, then some Nivea, then a wee and almost there. Just water to get now, to have by her bedside.

Hardy had grown used to the procedure, which had been added to over the years. At least she was not like his mother who had a mug beside her bed with her teeth in it. Joyce still had all her own teeth, just as Hardy did.

She had left her nightwear downstairs, so climbed into bed naked apart from her pants.

"What you looking at?" she grunted to Hardy.

Hardy turned over to allow her the dignity of not being watched while she climbed into bed in an unladylike manner. When the lights were switched off, it must have been nearly eleven o'clock. And as had become normal over the years, as soon as the lights went out, Joyce started talking.

"I cannot believe this situation."

"What?"

"Me in bed with you and a strange woman using my makeshift bedroom downstairs; we have another house; we have lots of stuff to sell, and we can hardly do a thing. It all seems so daft."

"It is daft, Joyce, the whole world is daft at the moment."

She forgot herself and rolled towards him: it was habit. She had forgotten the amount of light that came in from the street lamp just outside the window. She caught sight of the outline of Hardy's head – such familiar territory. Even the bed smelt the same as the last time she had slept in it.

"We're never going to use that house, are we?" Joyce asked.

"I'd rather sell it."

"What and then one of us buy a flat with the proceeds?"

He waited a few seconds.

"No, if you really want to know, I want to live with you till the day I die," he said. "The thought of life without you is not only terrifying, it's sad beyond belief. We argue, but that's preferable to not arguing."

"That's a nice thing to say, but why has it taken you all this time to say something like that? There's a lot of discussion to have, though, before we ever get back to normal."

"I have never been afraid of hard work and neither have you. The sale of the house will make life a lot easier."

"It's not about the money. I know I set all this crazy situation in motion … and I guess I could call it off. But only if you wanted me to."

"Course I do."

Silence.

"Night then."

"Night."

*****

252

If you enjoyed this book, you may want to explore other books by David Gary:

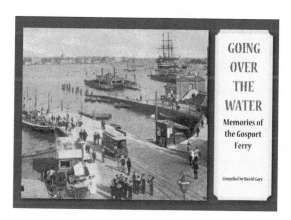